Contents

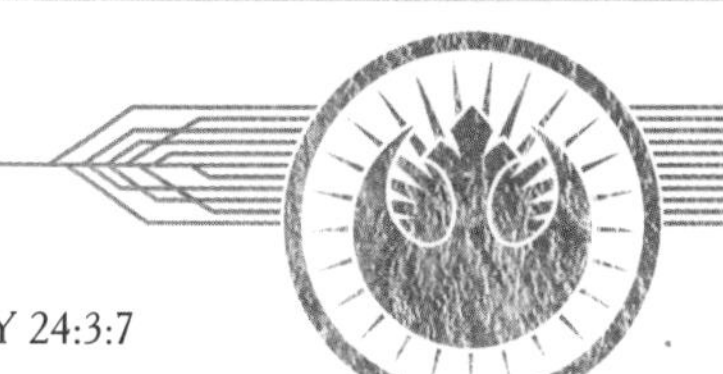

Yavin Praxeum, ABY 24:3:7

The Jedi Path is one of the most amazing discoveries made since the opening of the new Jedi Academy. It was found among the artifacts recently acquired from a Squib salvage scow near the ruins of Byss. While the Holocrons we've recovered contain more specific detail, this heavily worn manual is a tangible echo of a time long lost.

Our historians estimate the text was set down a decade or more after the end of the New Sith Wars in 1000 BBY. Its authors, Jedi Masters of the age, used the changed political structure and newfound peace as an impetus to codify the role of the Jedi Order, and to establish traditions that endured for centuries.

This particular copy of the book appears to date from around 115 BBY, and was passed from Master to Padawan in succession—some of whom I knew and some of whom exist as legends only. It is therefore of considerable historical (and personal) significance. The thoughts and observations of each owner are recorded in their handwritten comments scrawled on the pages—which makes for interesting reading. To the best of our historians' knowledge, the following is when each annotator possessed the volume.

- Master Yoda, the first possessor of this copy, apparently reviewed the pages for revisions in future editions.
- Jedi Thame Cerulian received the book when he was a child, and it remained in his possession at least through his teens, about 115 to 103 BBY.
- Dooku, Thame Cerulian's Padawan, took control of the book during his apprenticeship, around 89 to 82 BBY; he later turned to the dark side and took on the title "Count."
- Qui-Gon Jinn was the next owner, given the book by his Master, Dooku. Qui-Gon's comments appear to date from 82 to 72 BBY.
- We believe Qui-Gon kept it safe until Obi-Wan Kenobi received the book in 44 BBY.
- It then passed to Anakin Skywalker in 32 BBY. Anakin owned the book for a 10-year stretch until the start of the Clone Wars.
- Ahsoka Tano, Anakin's Padawan, held on to the volume, adding her comments during the Clone Wars from 22 to 19 BBY.
- Darth Sidious—the Sith alias of Emperor Palpatine—acquired the book during the aftermath of the Clone Wars and added his own form of caustic commentary.

I continued the practice of annotating the book's text, for I sensed it should remain a living document. Through its teachings, I have gained a greater understanding of what it means to be a Jedi and am honored to preserve its wisdom for generations to come.

LUKE SKYWALKER

THE
JEDI PA

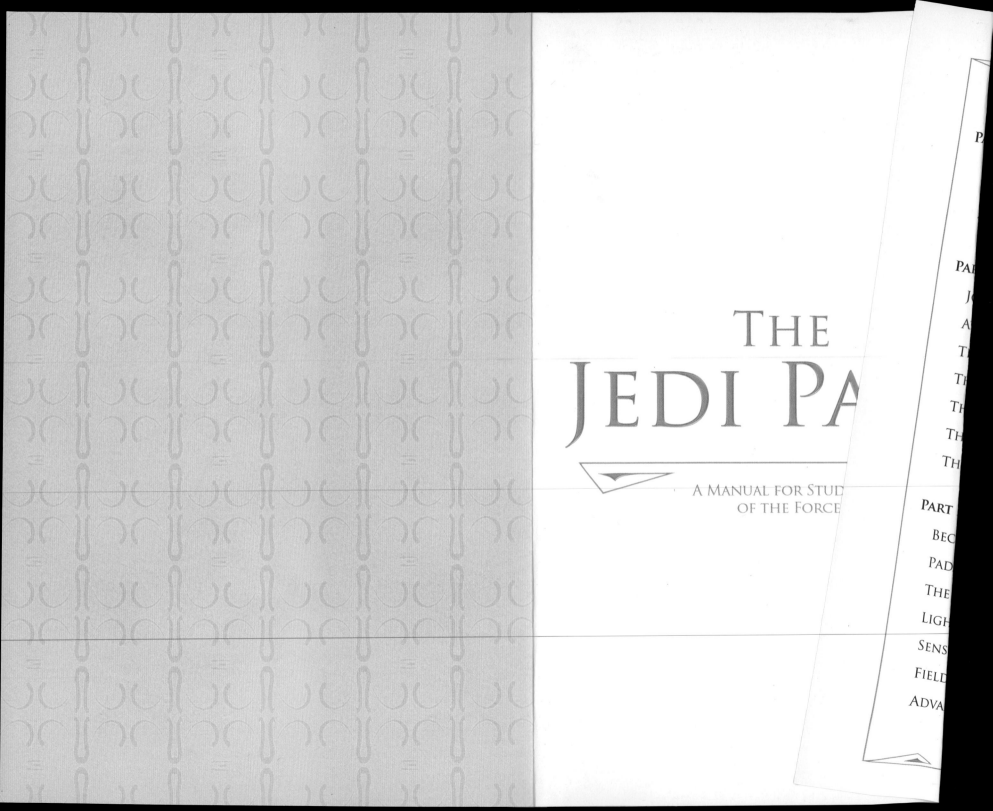

A MANUAL FOR STUD
OF THE FORCE

PART 1
INTRODUCTION TO THE JEDI ORDER

PART I
Introduction to the Jedi Order

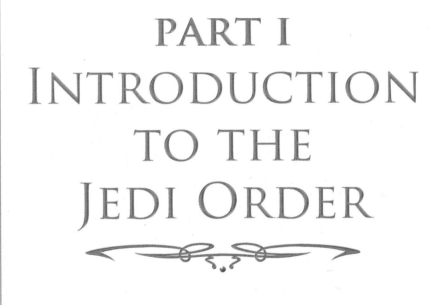

Remember Master Fae I do, from when I was a mere youngling. Good it is to hear her voice again through these words. —Yoda

YODA WAS A YOUNGLING?! —AHSOKA

THE JEDI CODE

BY GRAND MASTER FAE COVEN

For forty years, the Jedi Code has been my focus, as it will become yours. It is the philosophy upon which stands the Jedi Order. It is a pledge of protection to the citizens and inhabitants of the Republic. It is an encapsulation of our relationship with the Force. As a Jedi, you must be faithful to the spirit of the Code. Every day you must ask yourself: Do I understand it?

1.1 MEDITATION BRINGS PEACE, HARMONY, AND SERENITY—THREE OF THE FIVE PRECEPTS OF THE JEDI CODE.

OBI-WAN ESCAPED DEATH FOR A TIME, LIVING WITHIN THE FORCE AS A SPIRIT. I WONDER IF THOSE WHO WROTE THE CODE KNEW THE LITERAL TRUTH OF THE FIFTH PRECEPT. —LUKE

In its classical form, as transcribed by Homonix Rectonia during the Early Manderon Period, the Code consists of five core precepts:

If the Living Force engenders compassion—eventually even love—I do not feel these are a detriment, despite the precepts of the Code. Q-G

There is no emotion, there is peace. This principle guides all meditations and interactions with all others. It reaffirms the Jedi ideal to act without recklessness, and to view the actions of others through the pure lens of the Unifying Force.

There is no ignorance, there is knowledge. Those who don't understand this basic precept are quick to fear—and fear is the path to the dark side. The Archives represent the greatest collection of knowledge in the galaxy.

There is no passion, there is serenity. A subtle extrapolation of the first precept, this reminder to act dispassionately in every deliberation extends to personal obsessions and is a reminder not to elevate the self above the mission.

YES—MAYBE THIS IS WHY QUI-GON WAS NEVER ON THE COUNCIL! Anakin

There is no chaos, there is harmony. Those who cannot see the threads uniting all life view existence as random and without purpose. The Jedi perceive the structure and will of the many galaxies.

There is no death, there is the Force. All things die, but the Force lives on. As beings who exist as shades of the Force, the end of our existence in this form is not to be overly mourned. We are part of an energy larger than ourselves, and we play roles in a cosmic fabric that outstrip our incarnate understanding.

The Upper Manderon and Draggulch transcriptions add more—and controversial—tenets, but the Jedi need only to remember the core teachings to live their lives as gifted, yet humble, defenders of justice.

1.2 JEDI HOLOCRON

Updated, this section should be.
—Yoda

THE HISTORY OF THE JEDI ORDER

SO UPDATE IT, OLD ONE!
—DOOKU

BY RESTELLY QUIST, CHIEF LIBRARIAN

The Force is timeless, but we Jedi have not always been present to interpret its teachings. Centuries before the founding of the Republic, our predecessors first heard the Force's call on the Deep Core world of Tython. The seers of Tython knew the energy field as the Ashla, but understood it in much the same way we do today—as a source of wisdom, a regenerative pool from which to draw strength, and a way to move objects without touching them. Yet those seers who used their abilities in the service of hatred and greed fell into darkness. The Force Wars of Tython are the earliest recorded conflicts between the light and the dark, battles that would be mirrored over the centuries as the Jedi and Sith crossed blades.

WHAT DID THE DARK SIDE OFFER THAT CONVINCED SO MANY OF THEM TO REJECT THEIR TEACHINGS?
Anakin

CAN WE CARE? THERE'S A WAR ON!
-AHSOKA

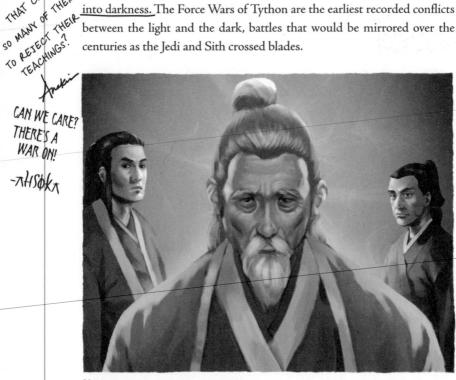

[1.3] QUI-KO IS ONE OF THE FEW SEERS OF TYTHON WHOSE WRITINGS ON THE NATURE OF ASHLA HAVE SURVIVED TO THE PRESENT.

1.4 THE FORCE WARS OF TYTHON, FOUGHT WITH FORCE-FORGED SWORDS, WERE THE FIRST CLASHES BETWEEN THE LIGHT AND THE DARK SIDE.

The Force Wars were fought with swords, their metal blades Force-enhanced for strength and sharpness. For even at this stage, the Jedi forebears had discovered it is difficult to wield a weapon that does not act as if it is an extension of one's own body. With technology from offworlders, the earliest lightsabers came into existence—and became the symbols of the Order.

No Kidding! -Thame

From Tython, the first Jedi Knights spread into the galaxy as proactive defenders of the light, settling on Ossus near Hutt Space. When the Galactic Republic announced its peaceful formation in the Core Worlds, the Jedi Knights vowed to defend its ideals of exploration, knowledge, and justice.

1.5 THE EYE OF ASHLANAE WAS THE CENTER OF JEDI CULTURE ON OSSUS FOR OVER 12,000 YEARS.

Ossus remained the center of the Order, but, during the Great Sith War, the explosion of the Cron supernova scoured the surface of that proud planet. Those few treasures that could be saved found a new home in Coruscant's Jedi Temple. On many occasions, war darkened our doors, including the infamous sacking of Coruscant by the Sith, which left the Temple a smoking battleground. Our resilience saw us through. The Order has at last defeated the Sith, following a war that lasted a thousand years. We now look to guide the Republic into its Golden Age.

Really? It appears that Darth Bane's philosophy of concealment was wise for its time.

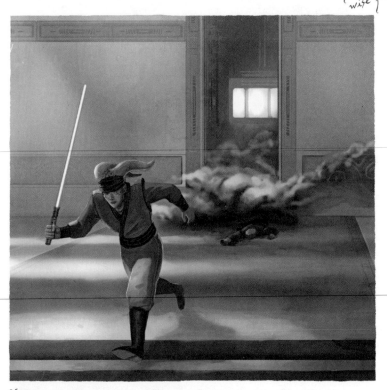

1.6 MORE THAN 2,600 YEARS AGO, THE TREATY OF CORUSCANT LED TO A SITH BETRAYAL AND A WEAKENED JEDI ORDER.

Structure of the Jedi Order

Typical Jedi inefficiencies!

Like armies and governments, the Jedi Order follows a hierarchy to aid in the flow of command. Though we are all equals in the Force, the more senior members offer an expertise that deserves respect by those who have not yet achieved such a station.

Jedi Ranks

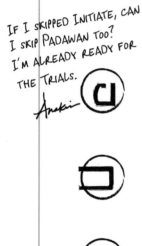

Jedi Initiate The youngest members of the Jedi Order. They achieve their rank when they are old enough for individual instruction, which for humanoids can be as young as age two. Training occurs in the Jedi Temple under the guidance of the staff and using the resources in the Archives.

IF I SKIPPED INITIATE, CAN I SKIP PADAWAN TOO? I'M ALREADY READY FOR THE TRIALS.
— Anakin

Jedi Padawan Initiates who, at the age of adolescence—twelve to fourteen standard years or so—are chosen by a Knight or Master for an apprenticeship. Their training largely occurs offworld.

Jedi Knight Padawans who have passed the Trials and are no longer bound to a Master. They are free to travel the galaxy in the service of the Order, and to take on their own apprentices.

Jedi Master Those who have trained a Padawan to Knighthood or have demonstrated the deepest understanding of the Force and the Jedi Order and joined the ranks of the Jedi Council. Grand Master is an honorific bestowed on only a few members.

Honored am I to be among its bearers.
—Yoda

The Jedi are more than 10,000 strong. Governance of the Order falls to the four Councils, one for each spire crowning our Temple's corners. The Council of First Knowledge guards our Archives and generously distributes its insights to our youngest Initiates. The Council of Reconciliation engages in peaceful diplomacy to end conflicts. The Council of Reassignment oversees the Jedi Service Corps, managing the careers of those who do not pass their Trials to become Padawans or Knights.

The High Council is the final authority on all matters of the Order. It is made up of our bravest champions and wisest minds. Under the guidance of the High Council, the traditions of the Jedi Order will endure for thousands of generations.

The council doesn't know everything. I know way more about smashball than Master Bouri!

–Thame

THAME KNOWS LITTLE ABOUT SMASHBALL. A FIVE-POINT DEFENSE MEANS NOTHING IN THE FACE OF A BYBLOS BLITZ.

–DOOKU

It's always easy to win when you play Master Dooku.

Q-G

WHO STILL PLAYS SMASHBALL?

–AHSOKA

1.7 The High Council tower does not set itself higher than the towers of First Knowledge, Reconciliation, or Reassignment. All four lie in the shadow of the Tranquility Spire.

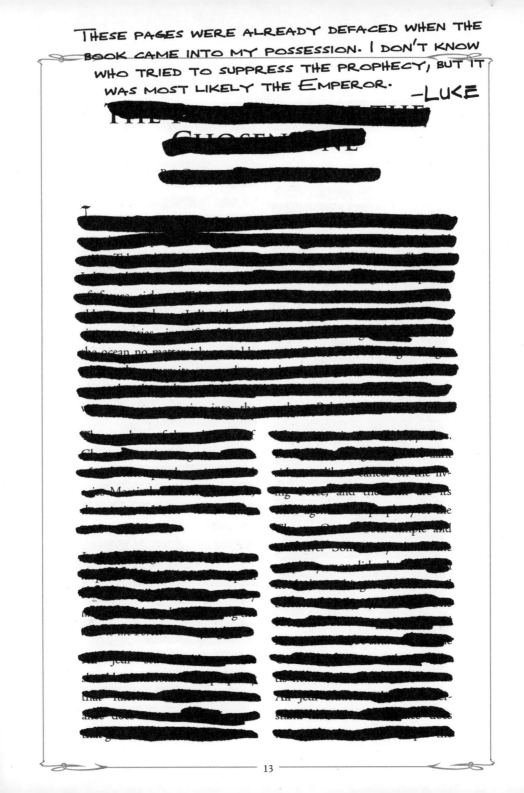

THESE PAGES WERE ALREADY DEFACED WHEN THE BOOK CAME INTO MY POSSESSION. I DON'T KNOW WHO TRIED TO SUPPRESS THE PROPHECY, BUT IT WAS MOST LIKELY THE EMPEROR.

—LUKE

elementals
fulcrum.

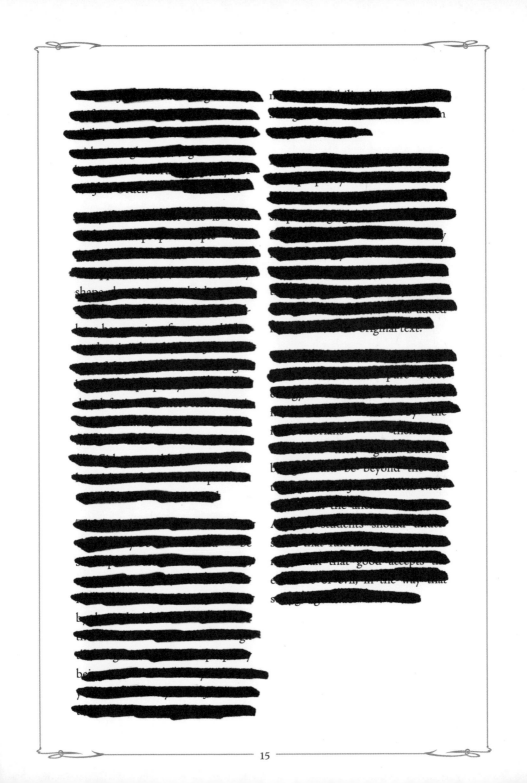

PART [illegible]

JEDI INITIATE

PART II
JEDI INITIATE

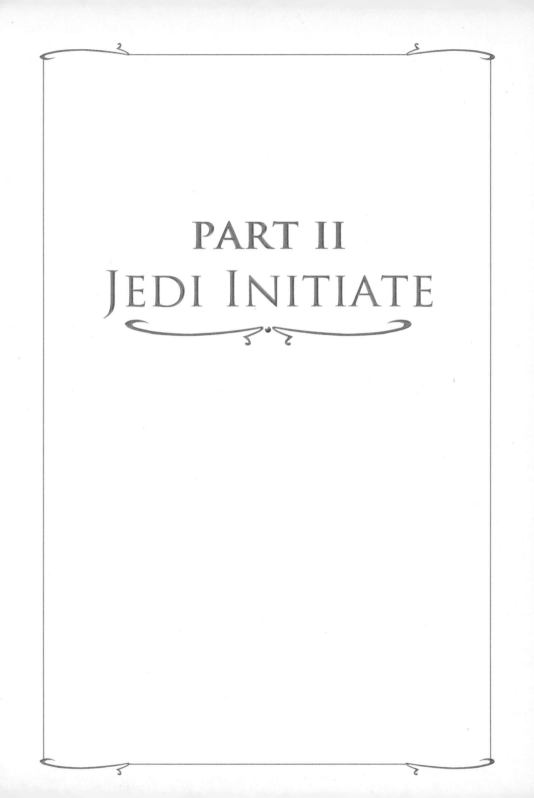

JOINING A CLAN

WHO NEEDS A CLAN? I MOVED STRAIGHT FROM OUTSIDER TO PADAWAN.
Anakin

BY GRAND MASTER FAE COVEN

This volume is an instructional guide to your life in the Jedi Temple and the service that awaits you when you leave. Heed the wisdom in these pages, but most importantly, pay attention to your teachers! Force instruction is held during morning sessions; history and politics at midday; and physical training in the afternoon. In addition, students must engage in five mandatory meditation sessions each day.

2.1 YOUNGLINGS FIND SUPPORT AMONG THEIR CLAN DURING THEIR STUDIES AT THE TEMPLE.

Younglings is what many will call you, including your instructors. Your youth fills us with hope; your developing skills fill us with pride. You are the future of the Order, so do not take offense when we point out your age. Take pride in your rank, for you are Jedi Initiates.

You do not face your challenges alone. All Jedi Initiates are assigned a family that will surround you from the moment the sunstone wakes you to the moment you drift to sleep on your mat. For most of you, your clan was selected before you reached the age of three or reached your species' equivalent in maturity. The Jedi fosterers who watched over you in infancy foresaw where you would belong.

SOMETHING I SHOULD HAVE TRIED FROM THE BEGINNING? NEXT WEEK I'M LAUNCHING THE RONTO AND VEERMOK CLANS.
-LUKE

No Thranta clan?
Thranta clan is the best!
—Thame

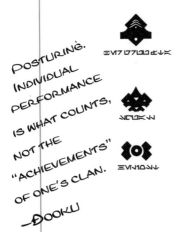

If you are of the Bear Clan, you are brave. No enemy is too fearsome for you to defeat.

WHATEVER. CLAWMOUSE CLAN IS THE BEST!
—AHSOKA

If you are of the Dragon Clan, you are tenacious. Nothing can make you back away if you do not will it.

If you are of the Katarn Clan, you are stealthy. You draw the Force around yourself as a cloak, taking footsteps in silence.

If you are of the Bergruufta Clan, you are loyal. Your heart will lead you forward when the way is dark.

POSTURING. INDIVIDUAL PERFORMANCE IS WHAT COUNTS, NOT THE "ACHIEVEMENTS" OF ONE'S CLAN.
—DOOKU

If you are of the Squall Clan, you are swift. Your tread keeps you many steps ahead of your foes.

If you are of the Heliost Clan, you hold great insight. Learn well the lessons of the Temple's lore keepers and no secret will remain locked to you.

These and the Temple's other clans are the roots of the tree that sustains us as an Order. Those of you brought to the Temple later in your childhood were assigned to a clan upon your arrival. You must never feel an outsider, and any reassignment requests to alternate clans should be taken only after the most serious meditation. These are your colleagues in the Force, closer than any brother or sister.

Until you are chosen as a Padawan Learner, you will sleep, eat, train, and grow with your clan. Jedi Initiates, never forget the bonds you make here.

CLAN BONDS MAKE BETRAYAL CUT ALL THE DEEPER.
—DOOKU

Attire and Comportment

By Morrit Ch'gally, Jedi Recruiter

Younglings who have grown up within the Temple hardly need guidance on what to wear. You've been wearing a uniform since you could stand.

The dress of a Jedi Initiate is essentially that of a Jedi Padawan, Knight, or Master. Tan or gray tunic, boots, belt—everything but the robe. The attire is not exactly the same as that worn by your elders, but it will identify you as a Jedi. When you finally step outside these walls to walk the galaxy, the same clothes you consider ordinary will be a symbol. People will approach you looking for wisdom. Others will beg you to fight their enemies. And others will attack you.

No—half the galaxy hates the Jedi, and the other half can be persuaded to ignore them.

Your uniform defines you. Wear it well and wear it with pride. When you sleep, fold it and place it at the foot of your mat. When you sweat through it after lightsaber training, wash it. When your boots are scuffed, polish them. Don't ask the droid to do it; polish them yourself. A dirty or wrinkled uniform will get you a reprimand from your instructors, but if that's your only reason

MUCH AS I WISH THIS WEREN'T TRUE, IT'S BEEN A STRUGGLE TO MAKE MY ORDER A WELCOME PRESENCE IN THE NEW REPUBLIC.
—LUKE

2.2 All ranks of Jedi wear special attire that marks them as members of the Order.

for taking care of one of your sole possessions, you don't appreciate what you have here in the Temple.

For those of you who are crystalline, or gas-based—or have a body structure that discourages standard clothing—you wear a sash, at the very least. Take care of it.

I'm a recruiter. I've brought hundreds of Force-sensitives to the Temple. Some of these younglings had already begun their first lives and were accustomed to soft fabrics, riotous colors, and endless choices—all the indulgences of the outsiders who value self over service. For these younglings, it can be hard to make the transition.

ABANDONED, YES—BUT NEVER FORGOTTEN. —DOOKU

Always remember that being a Jedi also means looking the part. Your attire is an outward sign of your commitment, and a constant reminder of your lifelong calling.

I only wish my room was this big. -Thame

2.3 YOUNGLING QUARTERS SHOULD BE KEPT ORGANIZED AND TIDY.

2.4 FOR THOSE JEDI THAT DO NOT REQUIRE TYPICAL ATTIRE, A SASH MAY BE WORN.

The core of all Jedi these should be.
—Yoda

THE THREE PILLARS OF THE JEDI

The Three Pillars of the Jedi—Force, Knowledge, and Self-Discipline—encompass all we do as Jedi and reinforce the precepts of the Jedi Code. Because the Force is in all things, it is rightfully set as the first pillar.

2.5 THE STATUARY ON THE FRONT STEPS OF THE JEDI TEMPLE IS ILLUSTRATIVE OF THE THREE PILLARS, A FACT NOT KNOWN TO OUTSIDERS.

THE FIRST PILLAR: THE FORCE

BY SABLA-MANDIBU, JEDI SEER

If you young students know anything, you know this: The Force is an energy field created by all living things. Even the pallie vendor on the megablock corner can recite that. It's a droid's definition!

2.6 THE LIVING FORCE ALLOWS JEDI TO CONNECT WITH THE PLANTS AND ANIMALS THAT INHABIT THE WORLD AROUND THEM.

It strikes me that the Living Force is the essence of our Jedi calling. Despite Master Dooku's warnings, I cannot turn away from helping others, even if it works against my destiny. Q-G

We Jedi are blessed with the gift of swimming in the Force in our every moment—breathing it, tasting it, riding its currents to our unique destinies. For the Jedi, the universe is never cold and directionless. The Force gives us purpose, and compels us to share our gifts with others.

WE MUST RETURN TO THIS IDEA OF THE FORCE AS IT FLOWS THROUGH US—NOT FROM US. —LUKE

Master Bowspritz will teach you of the midi-chlorians in our cells that channel the Force's energy. I urge you not to think too much on this necessary biological symbiosis but to instead cast your focus wider. After all, we do not drink the bowl but the soup contained within it.

The Force is bigger than all of us, but expresses itself in two aspects. The Living Force is raw and close at hand. It is the life energy tingling around you when you pass among plants and animals in a walk through a jungle. When beings die, you sense it through the

A shock I take pleasure in delivering.

Living Force. When many die at once, the loss of their energy may shock you, even knock you out. All of your tangible Force abilities—such as running, jumping, heightened senses, moving objects, or soothing the emotions of others—are techniques by which we become agents of the Living Force.

The Unifying Force is a vast cosmic power. You may not sense it yet, but with patience and insight you will. The Unifying Force is the stars and galaxies, the rippling surface of space and time. It is this voice that whispers of your destiny, and make no mistake—the Force *does* have a will. To commune with the Unifying Force is to temporarily leave your body behind, allowing you to walk in the past or see the future. Some of the ancients believe it is possible to even transcend death.

Too certain, Master Mandibu is. Clouded the Unifying Force can be and many mysteries does it hold.
—Yoda

2.7 The Unifying Force binds the stars and planets in space and time. Through this Force, a Jedi can sense the past and future.

What is the Dark Side?

As Jedi Initiates, you are young and have not yet experienced the temptations of the dark side. But take heed, for nothing else has the same potential to ruin your good works and good name.

[2.8] Jedi must turn away from the dark passions within themselves.

You already know of the Force as omnipresent, simultaneously existing as both a personal energy and as an imposing power through its Living and Unifying aspects. The dark side is not some "missing piece." Don't be tricked into seeking it. The Force is a mountain rising from the water—the dark side is merely the submerged, scum-covered underside. If you choose to dive, the slime will trap and drown you.

Passion lines the path to the dark side and must be avoided. Fear, anger, and hate are strong passions that will cause you to lose focus and to find appeal in the easy pleasures of the dark side. Love is also a strong passion and equally dangerous. Those who obsess over a parent, child, or lover devote all their energies toward the special object of their focus. The Jedi must serve all, not a select few. Should the urge to contact your birth families or form romantic attachments emerge, please consult your Master. To dwell in the dark will lead to suffering. Attachments will cause you to lose sight of your path and are cause for expulsion from the Order.

If you've spent time in the Jedi Archives, then you know the

MAYBE IT'S BECAUSE MOST OF MY CHALLENGES HAVE COME FROM SITH SPIRITS AND OTHER EXTERNAL THREATS, BUT I DON'T BELIEVE IN BANISHING ATTACHMENT. I CAN'T IMAGINE MY LIFE WITHOUT MARA, LEIA, OR EVEN HAN. —LUKE

I MISS PEOPLE OUTSIDE THIS TEMPLE AND WOULD DO ANYTHING TO PROTECT THEM. DOES THAT MAKE ME A BAD PERSON? Anakin

SKYGUY HAS A HEART AFTER ALL! —AHSOKA

ancient history of our Order. Before the formation of the Jedi Order more than 24,000 years ago, the people of Tython recognized the presence of an anomalous, yet benevolent, energy field. They called it the Ashla and learned to use it in the same ways your instructors are passing on to you.

Yet some seemed determined to ignore the will of the Ashla. They allowed emotions to interfere with their actions. They listened to the subtle whispers of the shadowed, submerged part of the Force. They called it the Bogan, and sank into its darkness. They never resurfaced.

Using Control Abilities

As Jedi Initiates, you will learn and hone many abilities that draw upon the Force. These abilities follow three themes: Control, Sense, and Alter. Control is centered on one's own body and is the focus of training for Initiates. If you cannot remain in control of yourself, you will never be able to extend the Force and command your surrounding environment. Sense and Alter abilities will be the focus of your training later, when you are more skilled.

The abilities that fall under the discipline of Control are basic skills, but improvement on these skills is necessary for the remainder of your life. Used properly, your Control abilities will allow you to survive injury and decay, extending your service to the Order by decades.

Control is overlooked by my classmates. They're too eager to throw things with their minds and push each other around. If I concentrate on Control, maybe I can outlast them all.
—Thame

Tutaminis, or energy absorption, is the ability to channel or diffuse potentially harmful radiation by using the benevolent energy of the Force. It can be as simple as shielding the skin from excessive sunlight, or as advanced as deflecting a blaster bolt with an outstretched palm—something that not even I have mastered.

DOUBTFUL. SOME ARE NATURALLY PREDISPOSED TO EXCELLENCE.
—DOOKU

Curato salva is a family of abilities that emphasizes the healing of self. When you draw on the Force to refresh yourself after Master Vaunk's combat sessions, you are performing the most basic position of *curato*. As a Jedi Knight, you will be expected to master this facet of Control to heal your own injuries, to flush mind-altering drugs from your bloodstream, to locate and burn out clusters of disease, to nullify the effects of poison, and to reduce your perception of pain when true healing is not possible in

Control leads to meditation breakthroughs. Count me as a follower.
—Kenobi

ESPECIALLY USEFUL IN A BATTLE!
—AHSOKA

the moment. The Jedi hibernation trance is the most extreme position of *curato,* and can be used as the last resort to sustain your vital signs until healers can intervene.

Altus sopor is the traditional term for the ability to increase one's focus on the Force. You can practice this self-directed ability during each of your five daily meditations. In time you will learn to merge into the Force so that you become nearly invisible to others.

2.9 *Tutaminis, curato salva,* and *altus sopor* are all self-directed powers.

THE SECOND PILLAR: KNOWLEDGE

Familiar a youngling must be with the Archives. From knowledge, wisdom grows. —Yoda

2.10 FIRST HALL IN THE JEDI ARCHIVES

RESOURCES OF THE JEDI TEMPLE

BY RESTELLY QUIST, CHIEF LIBRARIAN

SO FAR I'VE LOCATED ONLY A HANDFUL OF HOLOCRON DATACARDS FROM THE CHU'UNTHOR. SO MUCH KNOWLEDGE WAS LOST TO THE EMPIRE. —LUKE

The Pillar of Knowledge is the most important of the three pillars you will study during your time as an Initiate. As chief librarian and the caretaker of First Knowledge, I know this better than my colleagues. If not for the histories of the Order recorded in our Holocrons, what would Master Mandibu know of the Force beyond her vague feelings? Without the diagrams of combat techniques in our Archives, how could Master Vaunk know the proper way to instruct you in *shii-cho?*

As younglings, you should be well aware of the instructional tools we have in the Temple, particularly those in the First Knowledge Quarter, where you spend your time. Yet I am not blind to the inattentiveness and slothfulness that plague some students. If you have not paid attention to date, I trust you will do so now. Ignorance is shameful only

My classmate stole a Sith Holocron—temporarily, of course. The Jedi information resources are not as secure as the Council would have us believe.
—Dooku

if you choose not to correct it, and any question can be answered in the Archives or Holocron Vaults.

The Archives are the central knowledge base for the entire Order and contain more data than you could absorb in a thousand lifetimes. Its four wings are classified thusly: the history and philosophy of the Jedi Order, the physical sciences, the geography and political structure of the galaxy, and the nature and diversity of living things. To locate a specific datacard, query one of the droids or ask me or a member of my staff.

Next to the Archives and within the tower above the First Knowledge Quarter you will find the Holocron Vaults, which contain the self-recorded teachings of some of the greatest Jedi thinkers of the last twenty-four millennia.

Don't overlook other sources that surround you. The statues of Jedi thinkers that line the hallways should be known to you by sight, and the tapestries you pass on your way to mealtime depict battles and revolutions you can research further in the Archives. Even a place like the Room of a Thousand Fountains can provide you with an education in botany. Never neglect your mind in favor of your body or spirit.

2.11 Datacards can be used at any terminal in the Archives.

Is that what cards looked like back then? Funny.
-Thame

This is where I encountered those thieves who stole the holocron.
-Ahsoka

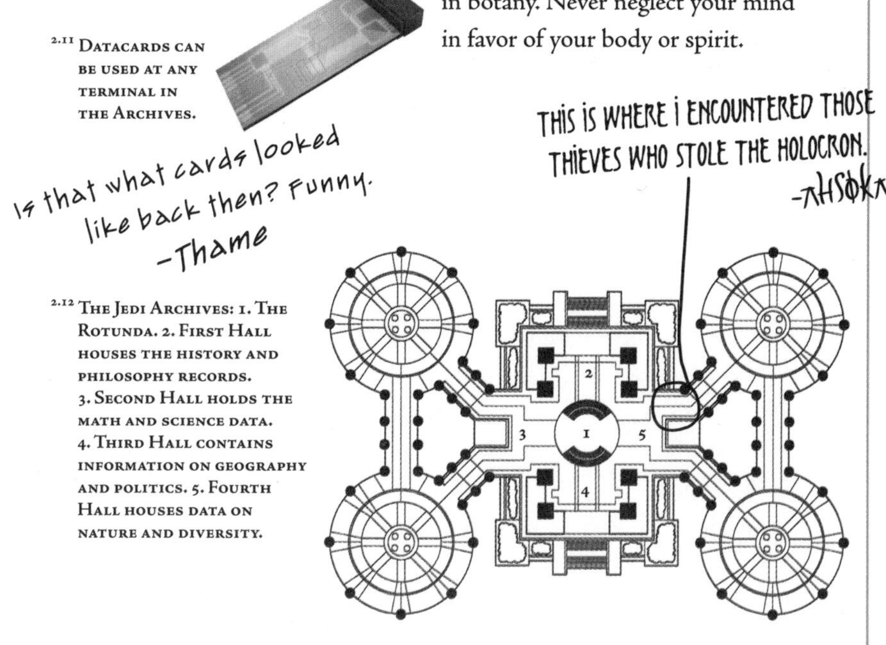

2.12 The Jedi Archives: 1. The Rotunda. 2. First Hall houses the history and philosophy records. 3. Second Hall holds the math and science data. 4. Third Hall contains information on geography and politics. 5. Fourth Hall houses data on nature and diversity.

THE GALAXY, STARS, AND PLANETS

BY CRIX SUNBURRIS, JEDI ACE

As younglings, your life is contained within the Temple. Until you're selected as a Padawan, your trips outside the Jedi Temple will be rare and short. So to prepare for that day, you'll need to study up. Beware that the Jedi Archives don't tell you the whole story.

The good news is, you're already at the center of it all. Coruscant is the capital of the Republic and the prime planet of the Core Worlds, located just north of the unwelcoming Deep Core. The next two regions, the Colonies and the Inner Rim, mark the outermost limits of what most citizens consider civilization. There's a lot more to see in the galaxy, but exploring it may mean stepping outside your comfort zone.

EVEN NABOO ISN'T CONSIDERED CIVILIZED! Anakin

2.13 CORUSCANT'S GALACTIC COORDINATES ARE ZERO-ZERO-ZERO.

Beyond the Inner Rim is the Expansion Region—home to factory worlds that are mostly empty and decaying. Keep going and you'll pass the agricultural Mid Rim on your way to the lawlessness of the Outer Rim Territories. It's here that you'll find some of the galaxy's worst criminals, and it's here that a skilled Jedi can make a difference. All this territory can be quickly traversed on the Hydian Way, the Corellian Run, or the Perlemian Trade Route. Most of you won't get your own starfighter, but there's no shame in booking passage aboard a starliner—the Jedi are public servants, after all.

Where Jedi have a true purpose. Q-G

On the outer reaches of the galaxy is the untamed frontier of Wild Space as well as the Unknown Regions, where hyperspace engines can't penetrate. There are many dangers in these sectors, but you must not fear them.

As you grow, some of you may find yourselves assigned to a satellite training academy. Coruscant's Temple isn't the only facility for Jedi students, and some Initiates and Padawans can learn more under a customized curriculum. Even Masters like myself visit these sites from time to time. It's nice to have a friendly port to duck into when you're on the run from Zygerrian pirates.

THOSE GUYS WERE MAKING TROUBLE EVEN THEN? CAN SOMEBODY SHUT DOWN THE ZYGERRIANS ALREADY? -AHSOKA

The training academies on Kamparas, Telos, and Obroa-skai specialize in data collection and analysis for you budding geniuses. The Tython and Alpheridies academies promise deeper study of the Force for hopeful mystics. The academies on Rhinnal and H'ratth may be homes for the healers among you. And don't forget the Socorro academy for Jedi Guardians—an outpost of order in a decadent and lawless world. That one's my favorite.

The Jedi were mistaken if they thought they could hide these academy worlds, as if this very volume didn't reveal their locations. My legions wiped them out, saving us a great deal of time tracking down the Jedi children.

2.14 THE INPUT LOCKS OF TELOS ARE THE ENVY OF SCHOLARS, BUT ARE ACCESSIBLE ONLY TO JEDI.

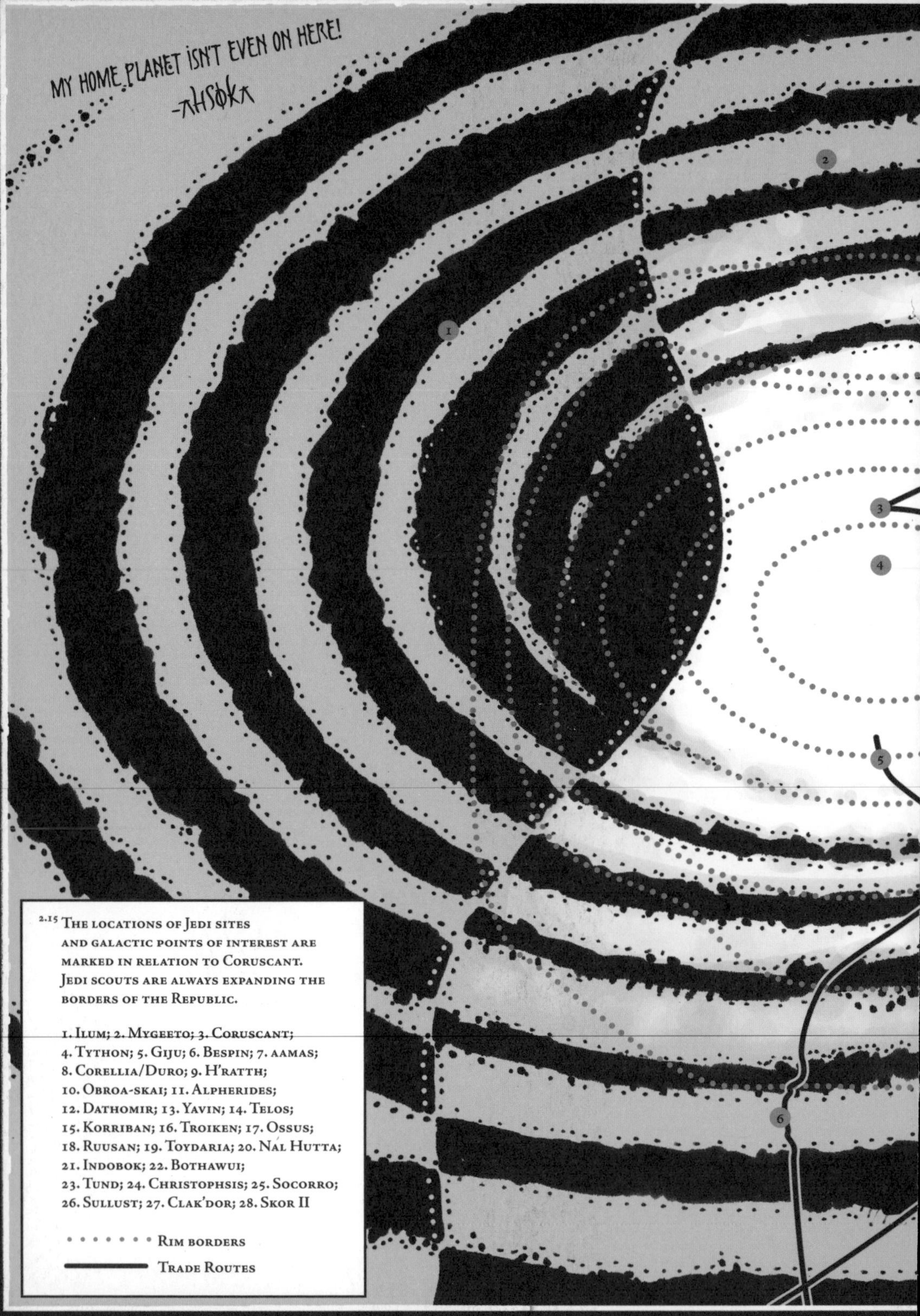
MY HOME PLANET ISN'T EVEN ON HERE!
-AHSOKA
1
2
3
4
5
6
2.15 The locations of Jedi sites and galactic points of interest are marked in relation to Coruscant. Jedi scouts are always expanding the borders of the Republic.
1. Ilum; 2. Mygeeto; 3. Coruscant; 4. Tython; 5. Giju; 6. Bespin; 7. aamas; 8. Corellia/Duro; 9. H'ratth; 10. Obroa-skai; 11. Alpherides; 12. Dathomir; 13. Yavin; 14. Telos; 15. Korriban; 16. Troiken; 17. Ossus; 18. Ruusan; 19. Toydaria; 20. Nál Hutta; 21. Indobok; 22. Bothawui; 23. Tund; 24. Christophsis; 25. Socorro; 26. Sullust; 27. Clak'dor; 28. Skor II
Rim borders
Trade Routes

SITE OF MY NEW JEDI ORDER.
-LUKE
14
16
15
13
12
17
11
10
23
7
9
18
8
19
20
22
21
24
25
26
27
28

GALACTIC BESTIARY

BY BOWSPRITZ, JEDI BIOLOGIST

Master Qui-Gon has always tried to impress upon me the importance of reaching out. But my patience is tested whenever we attract a gaggle of pathetic life-forms, which is often.
-Kenobi

Be thankful you can sense the Living Force, young Initiates. Outside the Jedi Temple you will discover an infinite variety of life-forms that contribute to the universal energy field. All of them are worthy of a Jedi's protection. Xenobiology is a fascinating specialization!

Animals are what most call living creatures not outwardly capable of speech or mathematics. As a Jedi, you will sense that this distinction isn't so simple. Most beasts *do* speak, if only among their own kind, and communicating in their tongue is a talent you can master. What follows is a sampling of the types of creatures you might encounter, but more information is always available in the Archives.

Creatures can be found to exist in nearly any environment—if there's one thing I'm certain of, it's that the Force always finds a way. Amid the towering ice crystals of Mygeeto, you'll find *pertorqus candus*—Mygeetan whiteworms—coiled in caves where their skin absorbs geothermal heat from the planet's core and converts it to food energy.

The jungle world of Troiken hosts the indictidile, a spiked insect that curls into a ball and impales its prey by rolling wildly through the undergrowth.

WHY AM I NOT SURPRISED? MAKE SOME FRIENDS!
-AHSOKA

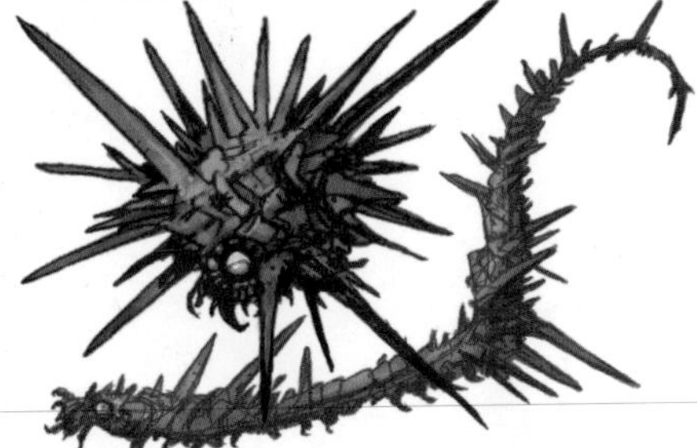

2.16 TROIKEN INDICTIDILE

2.17 MYGEETAN WHITEWORM

Life in all its variety is an infinite source of fascination. Q-G

2.18 Jodakan Needler Crab

As a Padawan, I once conducted a month-long study of the Jodakan needler crab, measuring its dart-firing accuracy and vastly improving the centuries-old data that was gathering dust in the Jedi Archives. For an illuminating example of pan-species cooperation, don't miss the moon of Alchenaut, where palm-sized furballs that I named o'cerrys act as a predator warning system for thousands of other herbivores. Even deep space harbors life—you'll never forget your first glimpse of an exogorth or a giant neebray manta.

All these creatures are bound together by one thing—the Force. (If this was not your first thought, you might be in the wrong Temple.) Even life-forms without midichlorians and cellular structures, such as the fractal urchins of Protogeyser, can touch its energy. Other creatures can do even more remarkable things, such as projecting bubbles that push the Force away, but the Council has quarantined such worlds, and full instruction on these creatures will come when you are older.

Why tell us now then?

-Thame

2.19 O'cerry

THE THIRD PILLAR: SELF-DISCIPLINE

BY SKARCH VAUNK, JEDI BATTLEMASTER

Many of you Initiates are all too eager to rush into this field of knowledge, for this is where you get to swing a lightsaber. But it is called the Third Pillar for a reason. Until you have demonstrated your connection to the Force and your willingness to study and learn, you will never be admitted into my class.

For those who have passed that test, you will do well to remember that this pillar is Self-Discipline, *not* Combat. It is impossible to wield a lightsaber without first mastering the action of your physical self. This is why we give Initiates training sabers. By the time you build a real blade as a Padawan, you should have enough skill not to cut off your own arm.

Meditation is the key to aligning your mind and body with the spirit and will of the Force. As Initiates you should be meditating five times a day. That's not enough. Whenever you have a moment to yourself, even if you're standing outside a training chamber waiting for a session to begin, center yourself as you have been taught. The Force will rejuvenate your body and sharpen your mind, even in brief moments.

You can practice deeper states during your daily sessions. Try to achieve Empty Meditation, which purges your negative emotions and lets you step back from attachment. Moving Meditation is an awake-state that reduces distraction and increases your focus on a task—you may find it improves

Highly recommended! -Kenobi

2.20 THE STILLNESS OF EMPTY MEDITATION ALLOWS JEDI TO CENTER THEMSELVES AND ACHIEVE A DEEP INNER PEACE.

your ability to repair a device, your skill in sifting through data in the Archives, or your combat drills. Rising Meditation broadens your connection to the Force, to such a degree that you may find yourself levitating. In this state, you may hear the visions and prophecies of the Unifying Force.

2.21 Jedi who enter Moving Meditation feel as if they can tackle any task.

Meditation is a daily expression of self-discipline. If you are having trouble isolating your mind, you can find several meditation chambers inside the Temple that shut out all external stimuli. You may also prefer the Room of a Thousand Fountains, where the sound of falling water is calming and centering.

I prefer one of the smaller rooms in the Reconciliation Quarter. -Thame

I accidentally discovered Rising Meditation years ago. When Han startled me, I was a meter off the ground. The fall wasn't painful, just embarrassing. -Luke

2.22 In the deep state of Rising Meditation, Jedi may find their sense of the Force increases and that their bodies rise from the ground.

Critical it is, to teach these skills at the youngest ages. Tra'cor, Boma, and Bear Clans, my personal attention will I give. —Yoda

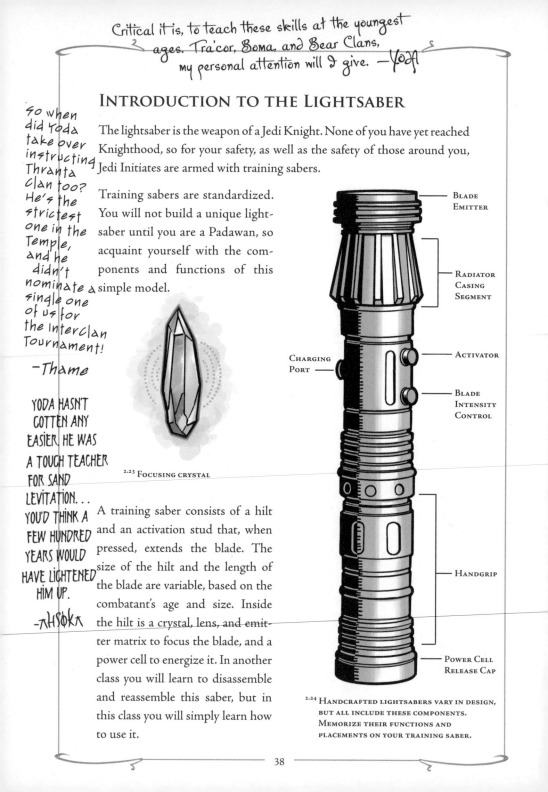

INTRODUCTION TO THE LIGHTSABER

So when did Yoda take over instructing Thranta Clan too? He's the strictest one in the Temple, and he didn't nominate a single one of us for the Interclan Tournament!

—Thame

YODA HASN'T GOTTEN ANY EASIER. HE WAS A TOUGH TEACHER FOR SAND LEVITATION... YOU'D THINK A FEW HUNDRED YEARS WOULD HAVE LIGHTENED HIM UP.

—AHSOKA

The lightsaber is the weapon of a Jedi Knight. None of you have yet reached Knighthood, so for your safety, as well as the safety of those around you, Jedi Initiates are armed with training sabers.

Training sabers are standardized. You will not build a unique lightsaber until you are a Padawan, so acquaint yourself with the components and functions of this simple model.

2.23 FOCUSING CRYSTAL

A training saber consists of a hilt and an activation stud that, when pressed, extends the blade. The size of the hilt and the length of the blade are variable, based on the combatant's age and size. Inside the hilt is a crystal, lens, and emitter matrix to focus the blade, and a power cell to energize it. In another class you will learn to disassemble and reassemble this saber, but in this class you will simply learn how to use it.

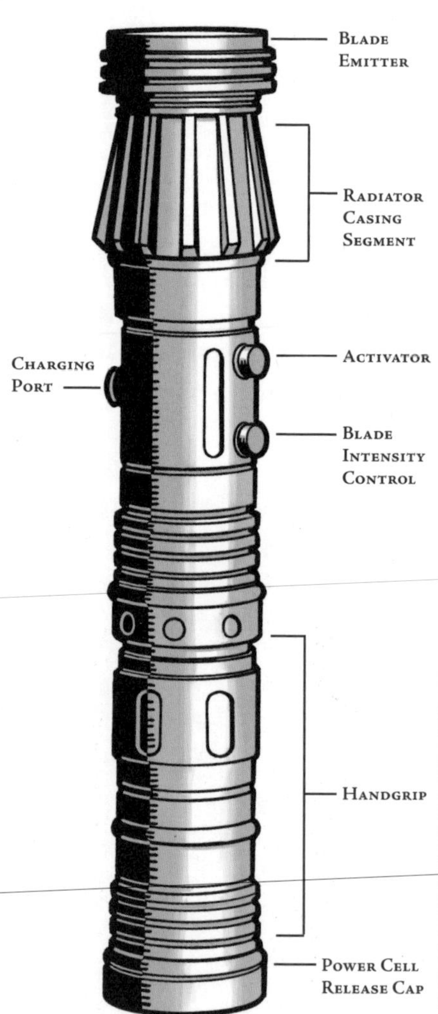

2.24 HANDCRAFTED LIGHTSABERS VARY IN DESIGN, BUT ALL INCLUDE THESE COMPONENTS. MEMORIZE THEIR FUNCTIONS AND PLACEMENTS ON YOUR TRAINING SABER.

The energy blade of a training saber will not cut; however, it is still a weapon, and it must be handled like the real thing. A hit from a training saber will stun nerve endings, burn skin, and singe fur. You will undoubtedly be hurt in your practice sessions, but a sore arm is better than a *missing* arm.

I NEVER USED A TRAINING SABER. I HAD NO PROBLEM GOING STRAIGHT TO A REAL SABER.

Anakin

THIS ISN'T THE ONLY WAY
TO HOLD A LIGHTSABER.
-AHSOKA

2.25 A STANDARD TWO-HANDED HUMANOID GRIP IS RECOMMENDED FOR YOUNGLINGS, FOR ITS STABILITY.

The uses of a lightsaber are many, for it is a tool not limited to combat. A lightsaber can form a shield to intercept and deflect incoming blaster fire. It can cut through bulkheads and hatchways. It can evaporate liquids and illuminate dark passageways. During the hours you're allowed to handle a training saber, treat it with respect. One day this weapon will save your life.

However, until you can complete the *sevinte* cadence with your strikes coming within a handsbreadth of your opponent, you are not ready for a real saber. To reach that point you must immerse yourself in the Force and practice, practice, practice.

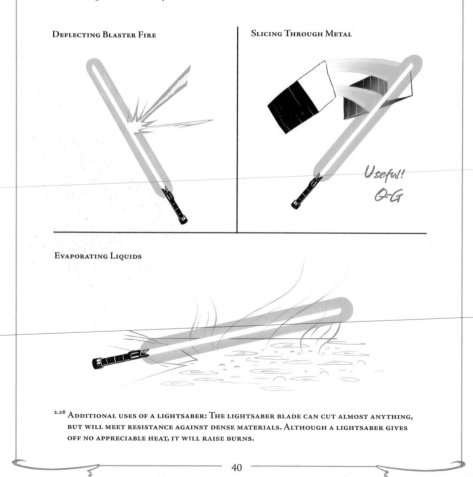

Deflecting Blaster Fire

Slicing Through Metal

Useful!
Q-G

Evaporating Liquids

2.26 Additional uses of a lightsaber: The lightsaber blade can cut almost anything, but will meet resistance against dense materials. Although a lightsaber gives off no appreciable heat, it will raise burns.

Form I Combat

There are seven forms of lightsaber combat. As Jedi Initiates, you will concentrate on only one. Form I, or *shii-cho*, is the oldest of all forms and the first to evolve from the ancient discipline of swordfighting.

Also known as the Determination Form or the Way of the Sarlacc, Form I teaches the basic moves of attack and parry, focusing on the humanoid body's target zones: left side, right side, head, and legs. It doesn't matter if your body is spherical, segmented, or serpentine—if you can manipulate a saber, you can master Form I.

AN UNFORTUNATE ANIMAL TO BE NAMED FOR.
-LUKE

SEEMS TOO SIMPLISTIC TO
BE ALL THAT EFFECTIVE.
Anakin

2.27 On a humanoid, Form I target zones include the head, left and right sides, and legs.

2.28 Practicing with a training remote is the first step in learning Form I.

Form I is the foundation upon which the remaining forms build. It is not the best style for blaster deflection or for lightsaber-to-lightsaber dueling, but it's a superior all-around form you can fall back on in the heat of combat. Thus, you must demonstrate a mastery of this form before you can continue.

During classes you will run velocities—a quick sequence of moves executed against an opponent until one of you concedes with a call of "Solah!" During such contests,

Another Jedi weakness—the Sith need no word for surrender.

2.29 The Form I velocity consists of six fluid moves.

victory can be quickly achieved with a disarming strike, or *shiim*. This inflicts a superficial wound on your opponent, causing him or her to drop the weapon or to temporarily experience a numb limb. Because of a training saber's inability to cut through body parts, this is the only one of the Marks of Contact you will learn at this stage. Deflecting the bolts fired by a training remote is another focus of daily drilling, one that will prepare you for Form V, should you choose to specialize in that style.

Although I am a Jedi Battlemaster, I must stress that aggression is never the way of the Jedi. More fundamental than even Form I is Form Zero—finding a nonviolent solution to any problem you encounter. In the words of the Tythonese Sky Judge Culoph, "the best blades are kept in their sheaths."

Wise Master Yaunk is. For knowledge and defense a Jedi uses the Force, never for attack. —Yoda

IF YOU NEVER USE YOUR SABER, THEN WHY HAVE ONE?

Anakin

THIS IS SIMILAR TO THE VELOCITIES BEN TAUGHT ME.

-LUKE

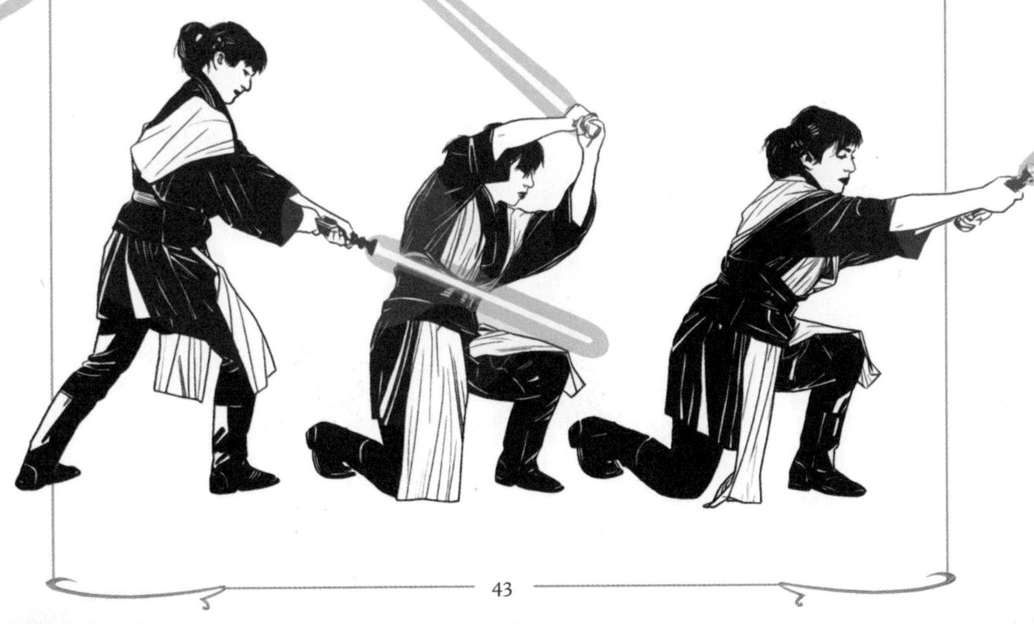

The Initiate Trials

By Grand Master Fae Coven

When you reach the end of your years as Jedi Initiates, you will no longer be younglings, and can no longer remain in the Temple. Without growth, there is death. All of you must pass from Initiate into a new level of service.

To reach this new level, you must complete the Initiate Trials. You should be well prepared for them at this stage.

- You must demonstrate your knowledge and understanding of the Jedi Code.
- You must also demonstrate self-discipline through meditation and lightsaber combat.
- You must prove that the Force flows through you and that you are not a rock stubbornly blocking its current.

Demonstrate an understanding of all three a youngling must, or ready to be a Padawan they are not. —Yoda

All these things are to be expected of one who has completed the training of a Jedi Initiate, but not all of you will pass through to the same place.

Some of you will graduate from Initiate to Padawan. This will see you apprenticed to a Jedi Knight or Master, and is a necessary step in becoming a Knight or Master yourself. But competency at the Initiate Trials is not enough to earn a Padawan apprenticeship. You must forge a bond with a Knight or

2.30 A Jedi Initiate must display self-discipline through lightsaber combat.

2.31 Paths of a Jedi Initiate: 1. Initiates may become Padawans; 2. Initiates can enter into the Jedi Service Corps; 3. Initiates should be prepared for the possibility of leaving the Order entirely.

Master, and some of you will discover that the Force does not wish you to follow such a path. Meditate on it now, so you will be prepared should such a moment come to pass.

You have all pledged to serve the Republic, and the members of the Jedi Service Corps are no less Jedi than those who roam the stars to defend the weak. If you are not taken on as an apprenticed Padawan, a position in the Agricultural Corps or the Educational Corps will allow you to continue to follow the principles you have sworn to uphold and serve the Republic as you have vowed.

Some of you may not follow either path. Regretfully, the Council may decide the path of the Jedi is not for you. If you arrive at this decision yourself, then it is the Force speaking to you, and you are not meant to follow the Jedi Path. Should this be your destiny, remember your training as you build a new life, and seek out opportunities to be of benefit to yourself and others.

THE EXISTENCE OF THE JEDI SERVICE CORPS WEAKENS THE ORDER. EXPELLING INITIATES WITH LOW POTENTIAL WOULD IMPROVE OUR PUBLIC STANDING. —DOOKU

Wrong—the Service Corps are some of our greatest members. —Kenobi

So many Force users still loose in the Empire—all the failed Initiates who possess just enough knowledge to be dangerous.

TEND TO AGREE WITH THE ORIGINAL SENTIMENT. POWER SHOULD BE CONCENTRATED IN A FEW. Anakin

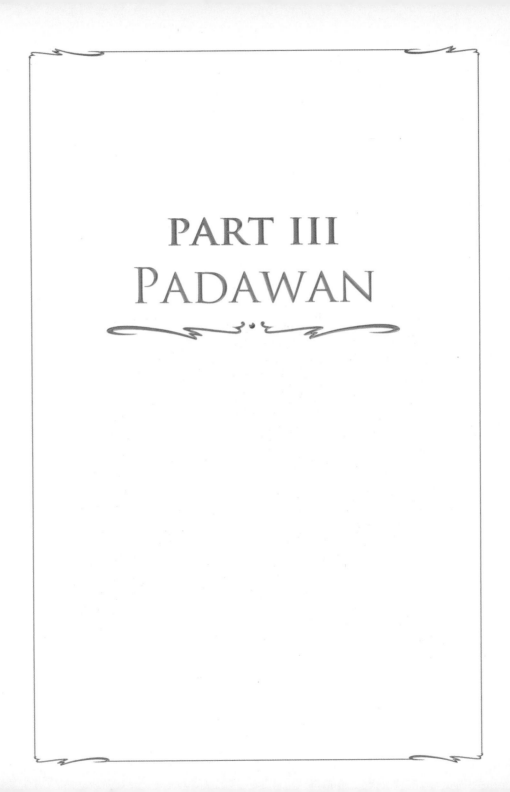

PART III
PADAWAN

I HAVEN'T BEEN FORMAL IN ESTABLISHING THIS STAGE AND TWO TRAINEES HAVE FALLEN TO THE DARK SIDE. MY FLAW? -LUKE

BECOMING AN APPRENTICE

BY GRAND MASTER FAE COVEN

As an Initiate you have learned much in the ways of the Jedi, but worlds of experience remain a mystery to you. As you progress from Initiate to Padawan, communal instruction from the Temple's teachers is replaced by one-on-one guidance from a Master. Not every Initiate will become a Padawan, but those who do will follow the call of the Force into a new level of service.

3.1 THE APPRENTICE TOURNAMENT ISN'T JUST ABOUT COMBAT. IT SHOULD BE USED TO DEMONSTRATE POISE, DISCIPLINE, AND FORCE APTITUDE.

My apprenticeship with Qui-Gon is hardly typical. ~~I can't believe~~ he accepted me after that incident on Bandomeer.
-Kenobi

When you reach the appropriate age (for most humanoids, between approximately twelve to fourteen standard years) and have passed the Initiate Trials, you are eligible to be selected by a Jedi Knight or Master to become an apprentice. One way in which you can attract the attention of a potential Master is through the Apprentice Tournament. Each year, the Temple holds a lightsaber contest for Padawans, which has at times included a free-for-all round or contests held underwater or in a zero-g chamber. Although the tournament winner will undoubtedly receive an apprenticeship, the tournament's true purpose is to demonstrate your individual style so that a visiting Master might assess your abilities and potential to be a good fit as his or her Padawan.

I HAD NO AUDITION. QUI-GON TOLD OBI-WAN TO TRAIN ME, AND I THINK HE RESENTS IT.
Anakin

For Initiates who aren't gifted in combat, the Apprentice Tournament may not be the best validation of your skills. Jedi Consulars who are looking for new Padawans often forego the tournament in favor of asking the Temple staff to point out promising scholars. Thus, if you are hoping for a good recommendation, it is best to keep this in mind when dealing with your instructors.

HAH—LOOK WHO'S TALKING! I GUESS I AM A WARTIME EXCEPTION TO THE RULES.
-AHSOKA

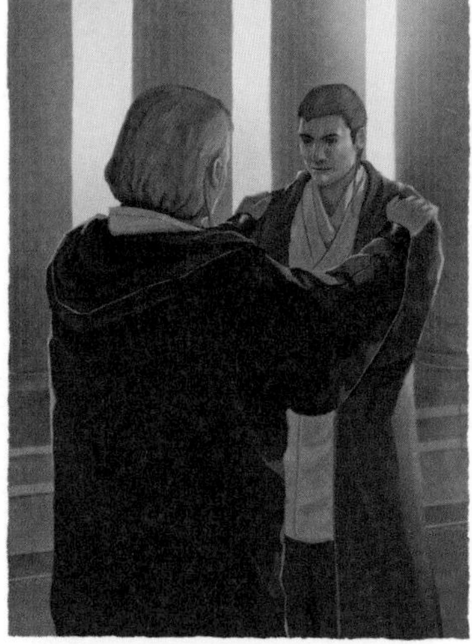

3.2 The bond between Master and apprentice is the basic structural unit of the Jedi Order.

The Council is generally not involved in the pairing of a Master and a Padawan. The Force will act as a guide, expressing itself through this bond, and rarely needs outside help. However, Jedi Seers have at times perceived destinies that require a particular arrangement of players. In these decisions, the will of the Force—and by extension, the will of the Council—must be honored. The Council's word is final.

Working with Your Master

As a Padawan Learner, you will venture into the galaxy far beyond Coruscant. Take this opportunity to delve into the Force and absorb the wisdom of a Knight or a Master who has long served the Republic.

Since a Padawan I was, a long time has passed. Challenging the expectations are. In many ways, the most difficult of the Jedi stages it is. —Yoda

The life of a Padawan is radically different from that of an Initiate. Your activities as a youngling were shared and structured, but as a Padawan, you will be executing open-ended missions and will be expected to keep up with Jedi who outmatch you in every way.

It is common for new Padawans to be tempted by self-pity, or to feel inadequate to the task at hand. These feelings will recede after a few months. Once you have established a rapport with your Master, you will be able to redirect your focus from yourself to those you are meant to serve.

The life of a Jedi is one of service to the citizens of the Republic, and your apprenticeship is designed to prepare you for this life. Outsiders may look at you with confusion, hostility, or awe, but you must focus on your mission. Your guide

3-3 Jedi serve to aid the people of the Republic. You and your Master may be called to assist them in an emergency or a time of need.

[3.4] A BACK-TO-BACK FIGHTING STANCE CAN MAKE A MASTER AND A PADAWAN UNSTOPPABLE.

through all of this will be your Master. Listen to your Master's teachings even when they seem contrary to what you learned at the Temple. You are an apprentice for a reason—if you do not seize every learning opportunity, you will never reach Knighthood.

Really!? -Thame

Some Padawans will find themselves apprenticed to a Master who does not share the same language, species, or even the same basic body configuration. These Padawans are most fortunate. An apprenticeship is for learning, and opportunities to recognize life in all its shapes merely affirm the Jedi's central mission.

Whether your Master is a mystic, a scholar, or a war-scarred veteran of the fight against the Sith, you must mold yourself into whatever role is needed for the mission. You are a Padawan—you must be prepared to do whatever is asked of you.

I don't know if I'm making a connection with Qui-Gon. He's so hard to read and the missions are far beyond what I prepared for. -Kenobi

STRANGE TO THINK THAT BEN WAS EVER LIKE ME—UNSURE AND QUESTIONING HIS PLACE. -LUKE

Padawan Attire and Conduct

By Morrit Ch'gally, Jedi Recruiter

Much of the Jedi success hinges precariously on the public's perception of the Order. Please don't make my job as a recruiter harder by looking sloppy and slothful.

Your braid is the most significant sign of your status as a new Padawan. For species with hair or fur, your tightly wound braid is grown behind the left or right ear while the rest of your hair is kept closely trimmed. It may also be adorned with beads or weavings. This braid marks you as a Jedi Padawan. It will be removed when you pass to Knighthood.

Seems rather restricting of the Council. Q-G

Why am I not surprised? -Kenobi

3.5 A standard Padawan braid

Species that don't grow hair may instead wear a woven braid of canvas or cloth around the wrist, neck, ear, or horn. Other alternatives have emerged over the centuries: Iktotchi Padawans can wear a metal circlet over the tip of their cranial horn. Sluissi Padawans can bisect their left cheek with a facial tattoo. Swokes Swokes Padawans can implant a medallion into the flesh beneath their foreheads.

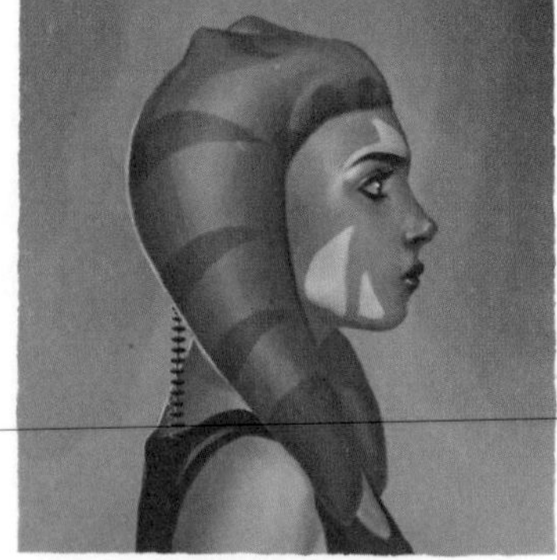

3.6 Padawans without hair may show their rank in other ways. Togruta Padawans often wear a chain of beads.

NICE PICTURE! MINE ARE SILKA BEADS. -AHSOKA

I like the looks Master Unskette and I get with the hood up! But the new haircut itches.
-Thame

3·7 A PADAWAN UNIFORM, SHOWN WITH AND WITHOUT THE OUTER ROBE, CONSISTS OF A TUNIC, BOOTS, AND UTILITY BELT.

Your uniform is another outward symbol of your status. It is made of humble, tough fabric, similar to what you wore as an Initiate, but its hooded robe makes it more suited for travel and exposure to the elements. Your Padawan outfit also includes a utility belt with pouches containing food capsules and comlinks, as well as other mission-specific tools issued by the Temple's quartermaster.

As a Padawan, you reflect upon not only your Master but also upon the entire Jedi Order. Remember to carry yourself with calm professionalism, to answer all questions directed your way, to be fair but firm, and to stay far, far away from cantinas and spice dens.

But you can gather excellent information in places like these.
-Kenobi

TRUE! I'LL ALWAYS REMEMBER CHEWIE!
-LUKE

THE REASSIGNMENT COUNCIL

BY GAL-STOD SLAGISTROUGH, AGRICORPS JEDI

Everybody thinks they know what a Jedi is—that we all serve in the Army of Light and fight the Sith Lords, or that we're all lightsaber battlemasters and starfighter aces. It just isn't so. Jedi can serve the Republic in other ways, too. The Jedi Service Corps is an honorable alternative for any graduating Initiate, and he or she should be proud to serve among its ranks.

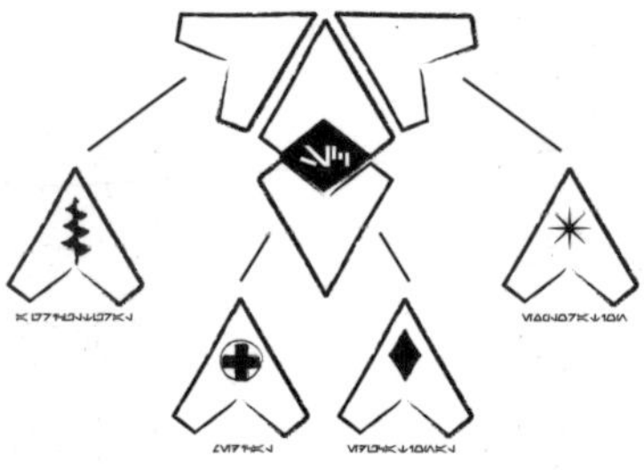

3.8 The Jedi Service Corps encompasses the Agricultural, Medical, Educational, and Exploration branches.

I was lucky to have saved Qui-Gon on Bandomeer and get a second chance. -Kenobi

When most Initiates hit early adolescence, they seek to pair up with Masters to begin their Padawan apprenticeships. If you are not selected, then what? You can try again the following season, but eventually the Temple instructors may tell you that you've run out of chances—and then the Reassignment Council steps in.

The Jedi Service Corps consists of four branches: the Agricultural Corps, the Medical Corps, the Educational Corps, and the Exploration Corps. The Reassignment Council, which assigns candidates to one of these four branches, manages the careers of these Jedi once they have been placed.

Not every member of the Jedi Service Corps failed to become a Padawan. Many Knights, Masters, and Padawans chose to work with the Corps because of their special talents—enjoying the best of both worlds, you might say. Still, the majority of those in the Jedi Service Corps received their postings from the Reassignment Council after several unsuccessful attempts at the Initiate Trials.

A career in the Jedi Service Corps lets you uphold the principles of the Republic in important ways. Some Jedi campaign for postings within a certain branch of the Corps in order to follow particular passions. It's a long and noble tradition.

I imprisoned the surviving Jedi Service Corps members on Byss. Even the strongest were easy to turn to the dark side.

3.9 Members of the Service Corps frequently work alongside Knights and Masters.

The Agricultural Corps

Violia got assigned to the Agricorps. Maybe I can visit her if Master Unskette has business on Dilonexa. –Thame

The largest of the Jedi Service Corps branches, the Agricultural Corps uses the Force to nurture and care for green and growing things. Accordingly, we are affiliated with the Republic Agricultural Administration, but we're Jedi, not bureaucrats. (Sometimes you will have to remind your peers of that fact.)

The principle behind the AgriCorps is that the Living Force exists in all things and responds to your will. Our enemies aren't exactly Sith Lords, but they're the foes of life just the same. Drought, blight, disease, and imbalance—all work against a planet's healthy biosphere and can be mitigated through concentrated application of the Force.

I suspect that Tahiri has talents in this field. I have no reason to start a separate corps but could blend the two philosophies. –Luke

3.10 The ability to control plant growth is known as *Consitor Sato*.

An admirable application
of the Living Force. Q-G

3.11 The denta fields of Taanab house the AgriCorps headquarters for the Inner Rim.

The AgriCorps is headed by a council of Jedi Masters with a special affinity for this line of work—lots of Ho'Din and Ithorians fill our ranks. Jedi Initiates sometimes serve brief rotations within the Corps as part of their instruction in the Living Force.

The majority of the AgriCorps consists of us lifers. Most of our work is based on Salliche or on the string of Core Worlds making up the Salliche Ag Circuit. But there are others stationed in the Mid Rim and on major food-processing worlds like Ukio. Jedi Geologists are a specialty branch of the AgriCorps, originating out of the need to study the composition of planetary crusts on unfamiliar worlds.

The most important quality for an AgriCorps member to possess is patience. Plants take a long time to grow, and rot takes a long time to eradicate. If meditation was your favorite subject in the Temple, then you may find the AgriCorps a fitting service for your passion.

WE COULD HAVE USED THEM ON TATOOINE.
-LUKE

The AgriCorps communes with the Force and encourages the growth of life by increasing Republic food production. Just don't take it too hard if sometimes the public forgets you're a Jedi too.

The Medical Corps and the Educational Corps

The second and third branches of the Jedi Service Corps are the smallest in terms of membership. Because healing and scholarship are already widely practiced by many Knights and Masters, there isn't quite as much need for specialists.

The Medical Corps is based right here in the Temple's First Knowledge Quarter. As part of the Halls of Healing, the Jedi Medical Corps Infirmary is one of the most advanced facilities in the Republic and is connected to the Galactic City Medical Center via private high-speed transport. Consequently, not all of its patients are Jedi. Critical cases are sometimes brought here for MedCorps ministrations, particularly to the Circle of Jedi Healers who report directly to the Reassignment Council.

The MedCorps is similar in function to the AgriCorps. Both groups use the Force to aid healing and encourage healthy cell growth. But because the MedCorps operates on intelligent beings, its members are also sent into war zones and disaster areas.

DEFINITELY TRUE! -AHSOKA

Among the MedCorps' biggest assets are the Healing Crystals of Fire. They're one of the Temple's most important mystical artifacts and are kept under constant guard by the Circle. It's said that the crystals can bring patients back from the brink of death when all else has failed.

MY STUDENT CILGHAL COULD HAVE BEEN ONE OF THE CIRCLE OF HEALERS. WONDER WHAT HAPPENED TO THE CRYSTALS OF FIRE? -LUKE

The Education Corps, or EduCorps, consists of scholars, teachers, and archivists. All Jedi are expected to be teachers to some degree, but the EduCorps goes far beyond that. They work under the supervision of the Temple's chief librarian and spend most of their days cataloging and translating.

No, these tasks can't just be left to the droids. Uncovering the layers of information inside a Holocron can only be done by a person with Force

3.12 Healing Crystals of Fire

sensitivity. Some of the Holocrons, datacards, and scrolls in our collection date from the eras of Ossus and Tython, and they are still giving up their secrets after thousands of years of study. The Jedi Order enjoys the fruits of this effort, but too often the core of the Order doesn't realize where it comes from. Within the Jedi Service Corps, a sense of humility is a valuable trait.

THE SITH HOLOCRONS TOO? THEY DON'T REVEAL THEIR SECRETS TO JUST ANYONE.
—DOOKU

NOW HE'S TRYING TO STEAL THE TEMPLE'S HOLOCRONS!
-AHSOKA

3.13 THE MEMBERS OF THE EDUCATION CORPS ARE THE GUARDIANS OF KNOWLEDGE—THE JEDI ORDER'S MOST VALUABLE ASSET.

THE EXPLORATION CORPS

The final branch of the Jedi Service Corps is the most far-flung. The Exploration Corps considers the whole galaxy its territory, and its members are rarely found in the Jedi Temple (save for the ranking Masters, who report to the Reassignment Council). Instead, small ExplorCorps outposts can be found in practically every Republic Ordinance or Regional Depots (ORD), some of them dating back 10,000 years.

These refueling and resupply outposts are used for staging expeditions into nearby space. The mission of the ExplorCorps is to uncover new planets, artifacts, species, creatures, and hyperroutes, and to assist any innocents they may find in the course of their adventures.

At each ORD base, the ExplorCorps team operates a few long-range scout ships, each light on armament but heavy on sensors and consumables. Members of the ExplorCorps are responsible for making first contact with any species that might join the Republic. It is a huge honor to represent the face of the galactic coalition.

Not every species is friendly at first, so the ExplorCorps sees the most combat of any of the Jedi Service Corps. It also has the highest proportion of Knights and Masters serving in its ranks. Some Masters specialize in the art of Force navigation, a technique that uses

A GOOD IDEA. I'VE FLOWN FAR TOO MANY LONG-RANGE MISSIONS IN A SINGLE-SEATER X-WING.
-LUKE

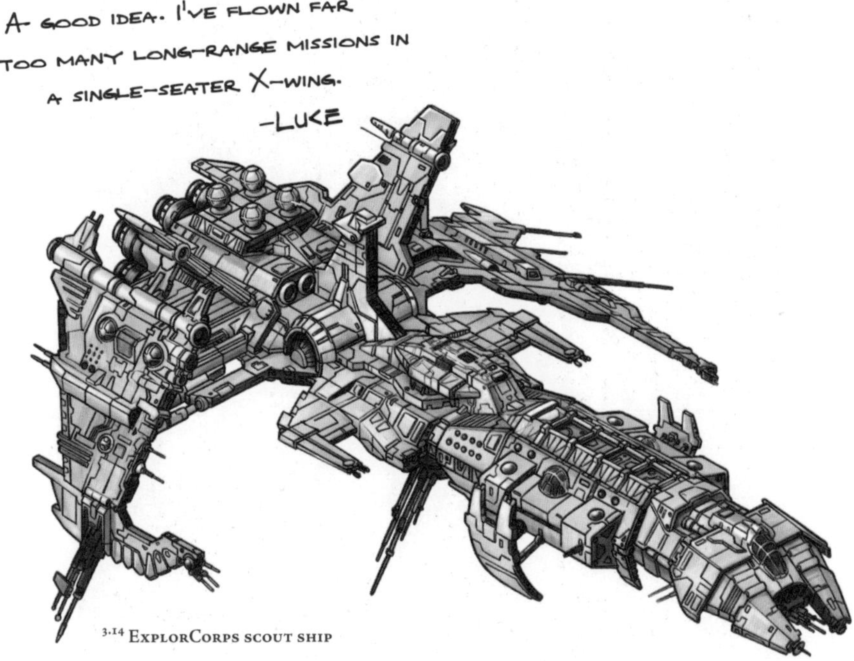

3.14 ExplorCorps scout ship

I have seen Master Saesee Tiin do this. It's remarkable! A bit beyond my abilities.
-Kenobi

outward-directed meditation to smooth the tangles of hyperspace and penetrate territories believed to be off-limits. The ExplorCorps is slowly chipping away at the expanse of the Unknown Regions, one system at a time.

The same foolish reason the Jedi thought they could succeed with the Outbound Flight project. I put a quick stop to that.

In addition to managing the ORD bases, the ExplorCorps operates a number of praxeum ships. Initiates who move on to a career in the ExplorCorps will sooner or later find themselves aboard one of these mobile training academies, where they can continue their education while helping out with long-term space missions.

The ExplorCorps is affiliated with both the Republic Survey Corps and the Intergalactic Zoological Society. The Academy of Jedi Archaeology is also affiliated with the ExplorCorps, whose members uncover relics and inscriptions that are then turned over to the Educational Corps for translation.

Outbound Flight's survivors are safe in the Redoubt. One more step in overturning this monster's legacy.
-Luke

3.15 By projecting Force meditation, an ExplorCorps member can maneuver a ship through dense hyperspace.

LIGHTSABERS: THEIR CONSTRUCTION AND USE

BY SKARCH VAUNK, JEDI BATTLEMASTER

The act of constructing a lightsaber forever marks Padawans as members of the Jedi Order. The construction of a lightsaber is more than an act of loyalty to the organization that has stood for a thousand generations. It is an opportunity to make a saber of one's *own*. The Jedi strive for consistency in manner and dress, but they do not make rules for this most personal of weapons.

Know themselves Padawans must, before a unique lightsaber they can build. —Yoda

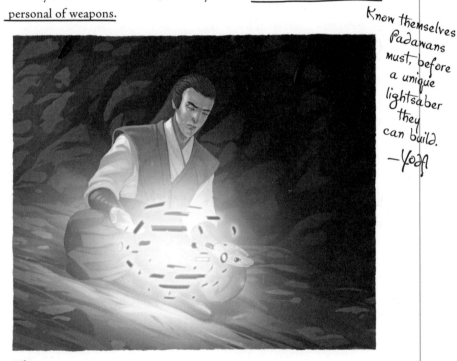

3.16 MEDITATION ON ILUM CAN TRIGGER HALLUCINATIONS, BUT IT IS ESSENTIAL TO THE CONSTRUCTION CEREMONY.

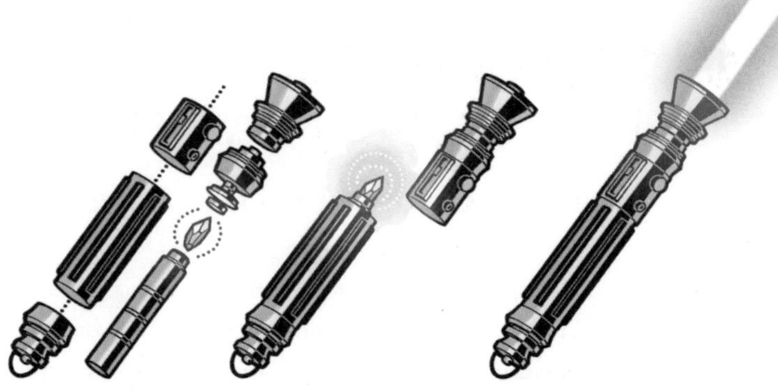

3.17 After the pieces of your lightsaber hilt are assembled, the crystal must be Force-aligned or the blade will explode or not ignite at all.

Components Your Master should have taught you to collect the pieces that make up the lightsaber: the handgrip, the emitter matrix, the lens assembly, the power cell, and the focusing crystal. Let the Force guide your selection. Should a handle carved from greel wood or an unusually colored lens seem to speak to you, listen to that voice.

Be on your guard—native gorgodons have an appetite for carbon-based life-forms! Q-G

Vision quest Unless your circumstances are unusual (or desperate), you will make your first saber in the crystal caves of Ilum. This Jedi planet is the source of crystals that emit bright green and brilliant blue plasma blades. Meditation will help you select the appropriate crystal. You must memorize this mantra:

That's an understatement! Is the Council trying to kill us? -Kenobi

The crystal is the heart of the blade.
The heart is the crystal of the Jedi.
The Jedi is the crystal of the Force.
The Force is the blade of the heart.
All are intertwined: the crystal, the blade, the Jedi. We are one.

Don't know what the the fuss is about—I easily killed three of them. Anakin

During meditation, you may experience flashes of your future or insights into the structure of the universe.

Achievement The final step requires absolute concentration, and it is the reason behind the forced focus of isolation on Ilum. The pieces of the lightsaber hilt must be fused together on a molecular level. This is done through precise application of the Force. Fail to align them properly, and the saber may explode upon activation. More painful than the loss of your hand will be the sting of your failure.

THE GORGODONS ARE JUST HUNGRY! TRY GIVING THEM YOUR RATIONS NEXT TIME! -AHSOKA

Lightsaber Variants

It is rare for Padawans to construct nonstandard lightsabers during their visionary experiences on Ilum. Often, a variant design doesn't emerge until much later, after years of experience spent analyzing one's own fighting style and evaluating deficiencies caused by that first effort.

INTRIGUING.
—DOOKU

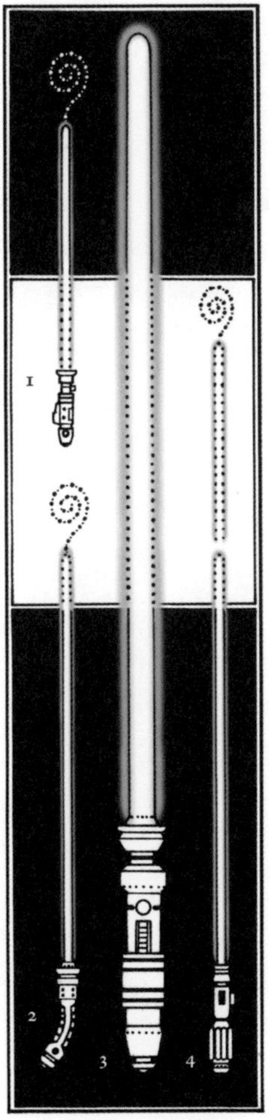

3.18 Lightsaber variants:
1. shoto; 2. curved-hilt lightsaber; 3. lightclub; 4. dual-phase lightsaber

- The **curved-hilt lightsaber** is perhaps the least radical of all variants. Its extended handle accommodates a slight bend seldom exceeding thirty degrees. This style is common among practitioners of Form II lightsaber combat, who prefer its balanced weight and precise handling for saber-to-saber dueling.
- The **shoto** is a short saber with a blade extending perhaps a half-meter. The shoto is often wielded in a Jedi's off hand as a second blade. The **guard shoto** is carried by means of a perpendicular handle, allowing for spins that put an opponent off balance but put oneself at risk. I do not condone the use of the guard shoto.

Carry a shoto, I do. Not a secondary weapon for those smaller Jedi.
—Yoda

- The **lightclub** is a giant-sized saber, with a massive handle and a thick blade. Lightclubs are often built by Houks or other Jedi of unusually large size.
- The **dual-phase lightsaber** uses focusing controls to shift between twin crystals, allowing a normal-sized blade to suddenly become twice as long. This is useful only for surprise attacks, and I have not found it practical for running saber cadences.

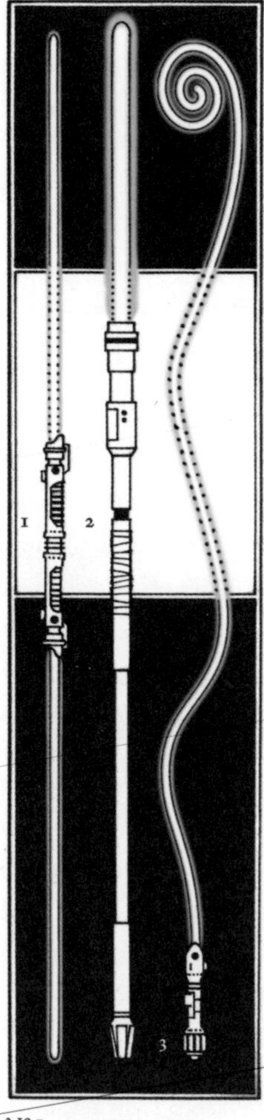

3.19 LIGHTSABER VARIANTS:
1. DUAL-BLADED LIGHTSABER;
2. LIGHTSABER PIKE;
3. LIGHTWHIP

- A familiar image from the last Sith War, the **dual-bladed lightsaber** is known as a Sith weapon, but there is nothing inherently wicked in its design. Using one takes years of study, and few Jedi—besides myself—can instruct you.

- The **lightsaber pike** employs the same combat style as the dual-bladed saber. Both are staff weapons, but the pike has a shaft of saber-resistant metal and a short blade on only one end.

TRUE, BUT IN THE HANDS OF A DARK SIDE MARAUDER IT IS DIFFICULT TO DEFEND AGAINST EVEN FOR EXPERIENCED MASTERS.
Anakin

- The **lightwhip** is the most exotic of all weapons that use the crystal energy technology. Instead of having a rigid blade, the lightwhip's energy tendril is flexible and can be wielded to entangle or cut. Unless you are already an expert with traditional whips, you should not even attempt to hold a lightwhip.

LUMIYA'S LIGHTWHIP SEEMS BASED ON THIS, THOUGH SHE HAD ONE WITH MULTIPLE STRANDS.
-LUKE

LIGHTSABER COUNTERMEASURES

Most people believe a lightsaber can cut through anything. That misperception usually works to our advantage, but all Jedi should be aware of the natural limitations of the energy blade.

Substances that can be fashioned by our enemies into antilightsaber countermeasures are the most dangerous. Study these and learn to recognize them on sight, and you just might prevent a nasty surprise during battle.

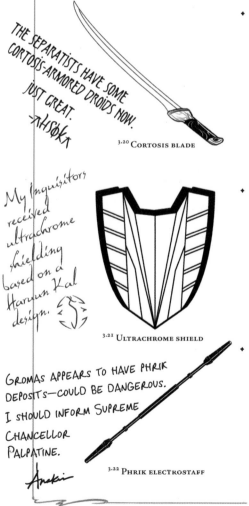

THE SEPARATISTS HAVE SOME CORTOSIS-ARMORED DROIDS NOW. JUST GREAT. –AHSOKA

3.20 CORTOSIS BLADE

- **Cortosis** This ore, mined on planets from Duro to Apatros, is the most widely available of all countermeasures. When used to create body armor or an arm shield, it can deflect a blade or create a feedback loop, which can cause a blade to short out. Cortosis is brittle, so on rare occasions, the power of your blow may crack this type of armor.

MARA AND I FOUND SOME ON NIRAUAN. I WANT TO ISOLATE THIS MATERIAL BEFORE OPPORTUNISTS START MINING AND SELLING IT. –LUKE

My Inquisitors received ultrachrome shielding based on a Haruun Kal design.

3.21 ULTRACHROME SHIELD

- **Ultrachrome** This superconductive material is worn by the Brothers of Barbeen, among others. The blade of a saber will diffuse across the surface of an ultrachrome shield, potentially melting its top layer, but an ultrachrome shield will stop any penetrative strikes.

GROMAS APPEARS TO HAVE PHRIK DEPOSITS—COULD BE DANGEROUS. I SHOULD INFORM SUPREME CHANCELLOR PALPATINE. Anakin

3.22 PHRIK ELECTROSTAFF

- **Neuranium** and **Phrik** These rare metals, when fashioned into shields or armor, can withstand a lightsaber strike. Neuranium can be chipped away over the course of a battle and eventually broken, but the time and effort required to do so may doom you.

3.23 Armor made of Mandalorian iron

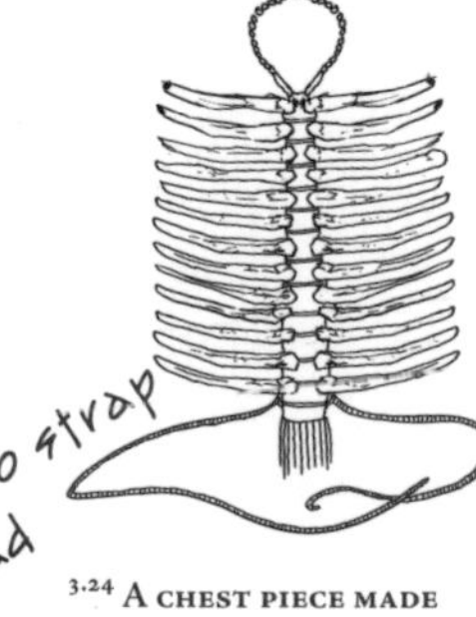

3.24 A chest piece made from the bones of a nighthunter

Who'd want to strap parts of dead things on their bodies? —Thame

- **Mandalorian iron** Also called *beskar* in Mando'a. This creation of Mandalorian metallurgists remains the most effective saber countermeasure by far. Sabers can barely scratch it, and a Jedi facing a *beskar*-wearing Mandalorian is advised to strike at weak points on the neck and joints, or to use Force shoves to keep the enemy off balance. Mandalorian iron is rarely shared with outsiders, and its scarcity is one of the Force's great blessings.
- The **bones** of some creatures, such as Onderon or Felucia, and **carapaces** of other creatures, such as taozins or fire-worms, demonstrate a natural saber resistance. Scavengers willing to pick through carcasses can exploit these creatures by fashioning bones into jagged blades that can withstand lightsaber blows—and by turning carapaces into crude shields.

Lightsaber Forms

There are seven forms of lightsaber combat. Form I was the focus of your training as a youngling. Padawans must extend their combat skills by mastering one or more of the following forms.

Form II Lightsaber Combat: *Makashi*

The second form of classical lightsaber combat, *Makashi,* is also known as the Contention Form, or the Way of the Ysalamiri, after a curious creature from the Inner Rim. This is the preferred style for lightsaber-to-lightsaber dueling, and it is the most elegant of the six traditional forms.

3.25 In a Form II duel stance, the feet should be in alignment.

Makashi emphasizes precision strikes and well-balanced footwork. A Form II practitioner keeps both feet, one in front of the other, on a line and advances or retreats along this line, avoiding the leaps and acrobatics of Form IV. It is a one-handed style, thus its adherents prefer using well-balanced lightsabers, including curved-hilt variants.

HOPS AND CARTWHEELS ARE FOR THE RABBLE. A COUNT OF SERENNO DOESN'T NEED TRICKS, ONLY A SWIFT DEMONSTRATION OF SUPERIORITY. —DOOKU

A successful Form II duel is quickly ended by penetrating an opponent's defenses and landing a Mark of Contact or a disarming strike. Skilled duelists are proficient in two Marks of Contact. *Sun djem* allows them to swiftly dislodge lightsabers with quick, spinning moves or by striking and burning an enemy's fingers. *Shiak* consists of straight-ahead piercing stabs that are a natural result of this stance.

3.26 The Mark of Contact *sun djem* brings an end to a duel by dislodging an opponent's weapon.

Form II duels are a respected tradition among those Masters who have earned the honorific of blademaster. Every year during Mid-Year Fete, blademasters exhibit their skills for their fellow Jedi in the exterior courtyard of the Jedi Temple. Marked by an opening salute and a blade flourish, duels are run until all challengers have been disarmed or have conceded.

The use of Form II experienced a resurgence during the last war, when Jedi Knights found themselves facing armies of saber-wielding Sith. *Makashi*'s fluid attacks and feints provided a critical edge during these duels to the death. Fewer Padawans have elected to study Form II in the years following the defeat of the Sith at Ruusan, because the odds of encountering a lightsaber-wielding enemy are now close to zero. However, I consider Form II the most disciplined of all forms, and I still encourage its study.

Wishful thinking! Master Qui-Gon's student has fallen and become dangerous. I fear more threats have yet to be uncovered.
-Kenobi

[3.27] In a lightsaber duel, the participants raise their blades in a salute, then flourish them before the fighting commences.

Form III Lightsaber Combat: *Soresu*

The third form, *Soresu,* also known as the Resilience Form, or the Way of the Mynock, is the ultimate expression of defense—and its masters are said to be impervious to all forms of attack.

Those who wish to study Form III are advised to practice their meditation, for *Soresu* is the most inward directed of all forms. You are to be the calm eye of the storm as your enemies rage about you.

Form III is the ideal lightsaber style for intercepting blaster fire and is common among ExplorCorps members and other Jedi who spend time on the Rim. A lone Jedi can withstand an ambush of twenty blaster-wielding thugs by dropping into Moving Meditation. By using this enlightened state, a Jedi can perceive the positions of each enemy and the moves necessary to intercept every bolt. Because this technique—the Circle of Shelter—is a precognitive state, prolonged use of it may open a Jedi's mind to long-term visions.

I like this! I'm already mastering control—think I'll be a natural at Soresu. —Thame

Therefore, when a Jedi is faced with a single blaster-carrying brute, a deflecting slash is advised. This technique catches a single bolt and swats it aside, giving the Jedi an opportunity to advance before the attacker can get off a second shot. Bolts can be turned back on the same vector from which they came, but this precision move is more commonly used under Form V.

When using Form III to fight another saber-wielding enemy, a Jedi should pull all moves close to the body and seldom make sweeps or lunges. This creates a strong defensive cocoon that makes it

THE SITH ARE BACK! THE JEDI CAN'T AFFORD TO WASTE TIME ON A PASSIVE FORM LIKE THIS. Anakin

AND NOW THERE'S A WAR ON. BUT IF SORESU KEEPS SOME JEDI ALIVE, ISN'T IT WORTH IT? -AHSOKA

3.28 Form III will keep you alive if you stumble into an ambush.

difficult for an enemy to land more than a glancing blow. But it means that a Form III master is unable to mount a counterattack. Yet the minimalist defense preserves the Jedi's energy reserves while simultaneously tiring an opponent, and an exhausted enemy will eventually slip up, allowing a Form III master to score a victory.

3.29 Opening stance for a Form III practitioner

Form IV Lightsaber Combat: *Ataru*

Ataru is the fourth form taught at the Temple. It is also known as the Aggression Form, or the Way of the Hawk-Bat. Fittingly, its kinetic moves require its practitioner to stay almost constantly on the offense. I discourage its study among Padawans, whose youthful energy too often translates into sloppy executions of the Form IV cadences.

Against multiple enemies,
only a true Ataru master
will prevail.
—Yoda

3.30 The Hawk-Bat Swoop

To an outsider, Form IV appears to be a blur of lunges and leaps. Its acrobatic style is best practiced by Jedi who possess talents for enhancing their speed and stamina through the Force. Even so, Form IV is exhausting and is best employed in short but devastating bursts. Thus, if you cannot find a way to penetrate your opponent's defenses after repeated efforts, it is best to withdraw from a fight you are not likely to win.

The moves of *Ataru* are numerous, and the style is more disciplined than its wild rush would indicate. Many moves are related to the Falling Leaf technique, which came into favor during the most recent war against the Sith. These include the Hawk-Bat Swoop—a surprise strike and quick withdrawal before the enemy has a chance to react. The Saber Swarm aims multiple short stabs at enemies to force them into a defensive posture.

To accomplish any of these moves, a Form IV practitioner must have mastered the footwork of *su ma*. Unlike other, more rooted forms, *Ataru* requires Jedi to use all axes of motion within three-dimensional space—*jung su ma*, a rapid spin; *ton su ma*, a somersault; and *en su ma*, a cartwheel. A skilled Jedi uses all three moves in conjunction with the Force to leap higher and jab faster than opponents can react, as well as to keep tired muscles energized until the end of battle.

Form IV is best used against a single opponent. Against multiple foes, a Jedi will need to adopt at least the pretense of defense, at which point a shift to Form VI is advisable unless you are a true *Ataru* master.

Doesn't exactly look like this when someone's flying at you.
—Thame

3.31 The foundation of Form IV is three *su ma* moves:
1. *Jung su ma* spin; 2. *Ton su ma* somersault; 3. *En su ma* cartwheel.

Form V Lightsaber Combat: *Shien/Djem So*

The fifth of the traditional forms is known as the Perseverance Form, or the Way of the Krayt Dragon. Its two aspects, *shien* and *djem so*, can be equally mastered by a Form V practitioner, but most Jedi express a preference for one or the other in the same way that most of us have a dominant hand with which we prefer to hold a saber.

3.32 *SHIEN* ALLOWS A JEDI TO REDIRECT BLASTER FIRE BACK TOWARD A SPECIFIC TARGET.

Form V is the most physically demanding of all combat styles. While Form IV requires speed and agility, Form V requires strength. Jedi without the natural ability to overpower their opponents should study another form. Conversely, Jedi of towering stature and imposing musculature may choose to focus on Form V, particularly because it requires less agility than other forms.

YOU CAN AMPLIFY YOUR STRENGTH WITH THE FORCE. WHY SHOULDN'T ALL JEDI LEARN THIS?
Anakin

The form came into existence through the efforts of Jedi Masters who believed that Form III, *Soresu*, did not allow sufficient opportunities for counterattack. From this idea they developed *shien*, a style that deflected blaster fire but redirected the bolts back along chosen vectors to take out attackers and other targets of opportunity. The *shien* Barrier of Blades technique creates a tunnel of lightsaber energy to ricochet enemy fire in every direction for maximum damage.

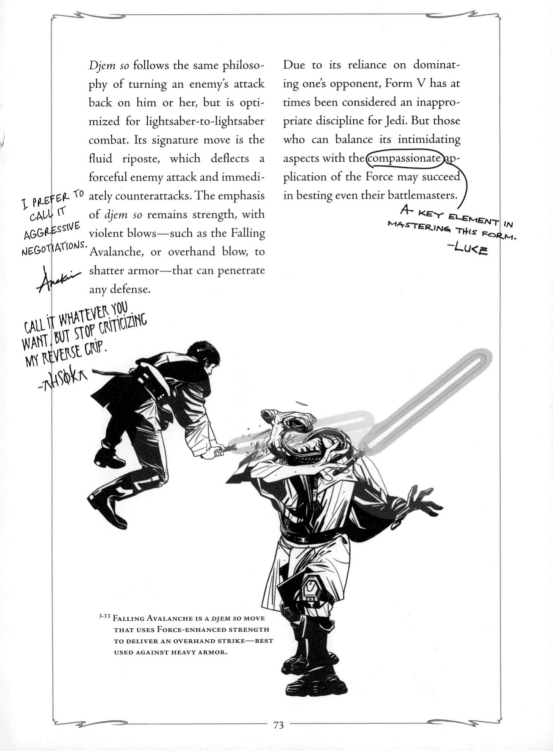

Djem so follows the same philosophy of turning an enemy's attack back on him or her, but is optimized for lightsaber-to-lightsaber combat. Its signature move is the fluid riposte, which deflects a forceful enemy attack and immediately counterattacks. The emphasis of *djem so* remains strength, with violent blows—such as the Falling Avalanche, or overhand blow, to shatter armor—that can penetrate any defense.

I PREFER TO CALL IT AGGRESSIVE NEGOTIATIONS.
Anakin

Due to its reliance on dominating one's opponent, Form V has at times been considered an inappropriate discipline for Jedi. But those who can balance its intimidating aspects with the compassionate application of the Force may succeed in besting even their battlemasters.

A KEY ELEMENT IN MASTERING THIS FORM.
-LUKE

CALL IT WHATEVER YOU WANT, BUT STOP CRITICIZING MY REVERSE GRIP.
-AHSOKA

3.33 Falling Avalanche is a *djem so* move that uses Force-enhanced strength to deliver an overhand strike—best used against heavy armor.

Form VI Lightsaber Combat: *Niman*

Niman, also called the Moderation Form and the Way of the Rancor, is the sixth traditional lightsaber form. In everyday parlance it is known as the "diplomat's form," for it is the style preferred by Jedi Consulars who have not chosen to make a career out of combat.

Form VI is the most balanced of all styles. It is not as precise as Form II, as defensive as Form III, as kinetic as Form IV, nor as dominating as Form V, but Form VI draws from all styles to create a hybrid form marked for its practicality.

Many battlemasters do not consider *Niman* sufficiently demanding. While it is true that it would be nearly impossible for a Form VI adherent to defeat an expert in *Makashi*, this doesn't mean that the style isn't useful for facing down criminals and thugs. Thus for Jedi Consulars, who devote a high percentage of their time to study and peacekeeping, it is a form easily mastered.

To compensate for the relaxed focus on bladework, Form VI encourages integrating Force powers into combat. Two notable moves include Draw Closer, in which a Jedi telekinetically pulls an enemy within range of a saber sweep, and Pushing Slash, in which a Jedi Force-blasts an enemy away after inflicting a cut. Proper management of these tools allows a Form VI master to take control of a group of enemies and eliminate them one by one.

It's difficult to use the
Force as a weapon while
trying to use a
lightsaber too!
I need more practice.
-Kenobi

3.34 In a Draw Closer move, a Jedi uses the Force to pull an enemy within saber range.

3.35 THE PUSHING SLASH REQUIRES A JEDI TO LAND A MARK OF CONTACT AND THEN USE A FORCE PUSH TO SHOVE AN ENEMY AWAY.

Niman is also the combat style associated with the use of twin blades. The art of wielding a sword in each hand is broadly known as Jar'Kai, after the Yovshin Swordsmen. Form VI acts as a foundation for this challenging practice. Those who wish to incorporate a second blade may wish to use a lightsaber shoto in their off hand, for its shorter blade allows for greater range of motion. Jedi who have multiple limbs, such as the Priapulin Master Skwelli, who carried six sabers, are a wonder to behold in the extant recordings in the Jedi Holocrons.

I AM WORKING ON THIS, MOSTLY AS AN EXERCISE IN CONTROL. I DOUBT I WILL NEED TO USE IT.
Anakin

I've seen this recording! He's amazing.
-Thame

3.36 WHEN USING TWO BLADES, FORM VI PRACTITIONERS HOLD A SHORTER BLADED SHOTO IN THEIR OFF HAND.

I TOO HAVE SEEN THIS RECORDING. HIS FORM IS SLOPPY AND HIS FOOTWORK IS NONEXISTENT.
-DOOKU

I shudder at the thought of facing that many sabers at once.
-Kenobi

Marks of Contact

Lightsaber combat ends when an opponent is disabled, dead, or forced to surrender. Such results are achieved through the Marks of Contact. The Marks of Contact should be applied with intent, and with the objective of preserving life unless circumstances force you to deliver a killing blow.

- ***Shiim,*** one of the two fundamental Marks, is a blow delivered with the edge of the blade. It usually inflicts superficial wounds, but if you have any opening in battle you should be quick to seize it.
- ***Shiak,*** the second fundamental Mark, pierces an opponent with the blade's point. Preferred for its precision, it is a Mark that indicates you are in control of the blade and the Force is in control of you.

VERY TRUE. IT IS THE SIGNATURE MOVE OF A MAKASHI MASTER.
—DOOKU

- ***Sun djem,*** as you read under Form II, can disarm an opponent by destroying his weapon or forcing him to drop it.
- ***Cho mai*** is more direct. It severs the weapon hand entirely, leaving your opponent alive but unable to continue the fight, and is thus a merciful conclusion to battle.

I DON'T KNOW THAT I'D CALL IT MERCIFUL.
—LUKE

- ***Cho sun*** removes the entire weapon arm at a point above the elbow on most humanoids. Not as precise as *cho mai,* it will nevertheless end a battle quickly.
- ***Cho mok*** severs a different limb, such as a leg. Maiming of this nature should be done only if an opening exists and you do not think you can otherwise win the fight.
- ***Mou kei*** is a forbidden variant, literally meaning "to dismember." It involves the act of cutting through several limbs at once. You should never need to use *mou kei* against a living being given the many alternatives.

I can't see ever using such a Mark.
-Kenobi

- ***Sai cha*** is the act of cutting an enemy's head from his shoulders. It is never the intention of a Jedi to extinguish a fellow life, for even the worst of us exists as a luminous being in the warmth of the Force. But when required, a lightsaber can also kill. If a *shiak* thrust through the heart cannot be done, this is the preferred method for a fatality.
- ***Sai tok*** slices an entire body into two halves. This act is rightly considered barbaric and evidence of the furious emotions of the dark side. Unless you're fighting droids, no student of mine should ever use *sai tok*.

THE OTHER PADAWANS SAY OBI-WAN KILLED THE SITH ON NABOO THIS WAY. I'M GLAD HE DID.

Anakin

3·37 THERE ARE NINE MARKS OF CONTACT A JEDI MAY LAND ON AN OPPONENT.

Sense Abilities

By Sabla-Mandibu, Jedi Seer

As Initiates you worked to master your body's reactions and to enhance your limitations through your instruction in Control. As Padawans, you will spend far more time developing the discipline of Sense and the Force abilities that emanate from it.

3.38 LIFE-FORMS MAY APPEAR BATHED IN LIGHT UNDER THE FORCE SENSE.

Sense is a natural broadening of the principles of Control. As you extend your reach beyond yourself to your environment, be prepared to gain a deeper, cosmic awareness as the Living Force reveals itself to you. Some of you have been training in these exercises for years, but as Padawans you should experience a breakthrough moment when everything becomes as natural as using your eyes to see or your ears to hear.

Life detection is the most basic of the Sense abilities. It is known in traditional High Galactic as *prima vitae*. Through this ability, you can feel the presence of living things and track their positions at long range. You may even discover that life signatures have unique flavors, with colleagues and friendly locals giving off a warm, reassuring glow that is instantly distinguishable from the anger of an enemy. The bond you share with your Master is

Each individual? Or their intentions? –Thame

the most important expression of *prima vitae* and provides a conceptual proof for how far your abilities might take you. Some Padawans can feel the presence of their Masters from light-years away.

The Living Force is what provides the link between all living things. Perceiving the totality of those strands is the object of *tactus otium* or **Sense Force**. To practice or hone this ability, do not focus on a single signature. Relax your perceptions so that all around you becomes a blur. The Force will reveal itself in time, letting you see an area's Force signature and revealing whether it is healthy or sickly, beneficial or malevolent. Some places are strong in the dark side; this sense will provide you a bit of warning before you approach such a site.

Have been practicing this. There's so much life, even on Coruscant!
Q-G

THE CAVE ON DAGOBAH?
-LUKE

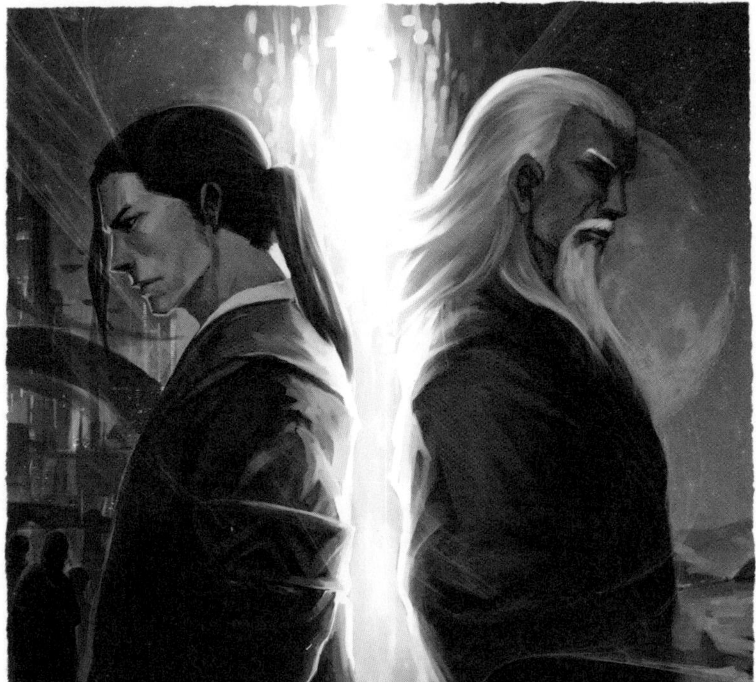

3.39 The Force is not hindered by distance. A Master and Padawan team can sense each other and sometimes even communicate when separated by many light-years.

Does the interrogation of a captured Jedi send a strong signal, too? We shall see.

I EXPERIENCED THIS MONSTER'S TORTURES. I HOPE THE GALAXY NEVER SEES HIS LIKE AGAIN.
-LUKE

PRACTICING SENSE ABILITIES

Magnifying the senses is an obvious application of the Force but one that many Padawans struggle to apply. Because the Force often supplies its own unique perspective, it can feel counterintuitive to use it for enhancing the same senses we use every day. Padawans who need help in this area are advised to practice Force-boosted hearing while meditating, with all other senses closed down. Program a training remote to travel away from you at one meter per minute. After listening to the quiet hum of its repulsorlift for a time, you may be shocked to discover that it has already left your chamber and is halfway through the Temple. Through this same technique you can gain improved eyesight that exceeds the range of macrobinoculars. If you are of a species that relies on scent, taste, air pressure, or electromagnetism, you can adapt this exercise to achieve similar successes.

Or just program the remote to eavesdrop! They can take holo-images too. Nice shortcut! -Thame

Shortcuts at the expense of training will make you a weaker Jedi. Q-G

WHATEVER GETS THE JOB DONE. Anakin

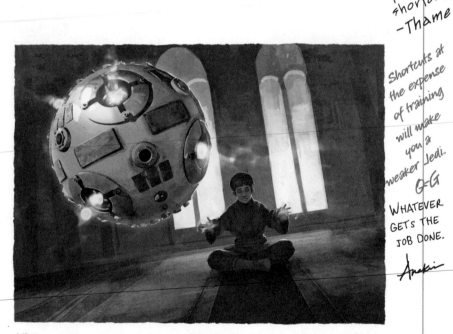

3.40 USING A TRAINING REMOTE TO PRACTICE FORCE-BOOSTED HEARING IS A FUNDAMENTAL EXERCISE IN DEVELOPING MAGNIFYING SENSE.

[3.41] POSTCOGNITION ALLOWS A JEDI TO SENSE THE HISTORY OF AN OBJECT, DEEPER THAN ANY RECORDING.

Postcognition, or *tai vordrax*, is one of the few Sense abilities that draws upon the Unifying Force. You are still extending your perceptions, but in this case you are doing it within the flow of time itself. The *psychometry* technique involves handling an object to get a Force reading of the beings who handled it last. This can also apply to a general area—to see what transpired in a particular room, for example—but works best for recent or violent events. This is not the same thing as Force-enhanced memory recall, because the Jedi need not ever have been present for Postcognition. You are drawing on the Force's memory of the event, not your own.

Master Tholme's Padawan Quinlan can do this. Amazing. -Kenobi

Projective telepathy combines your perceptual abilities of Sense with the more direct discipline of Alter, allowing you to actually put your voice into the mind of another. Even some members of the Council cannot achieve this, so don't be discouraged. It is far easier to give a fellow Jedi a general "warning" sense than to convey a detailed message including the number of attackers and the weapons each is carrying. On the other hand if you're a Hortek, Draethos, or a member of another telepathic species, take pride in your natural gift!

[3.42] THROUGH THE FORCE, JEDI CAN RELAY WORDS WITHOUT SPEAKING.

FIELD EQUIPMENT AND MISSION RESPONSIBILITY

BY MORRIT CH'GALLY, JEDI RECRUITER

As a Padawan, one of the hardest things to get used to is the amount of travel you'll need to tackle. Coruscant isn't your home anymore. You can find yourself on any planet in the galaxy, dealing with snow, sand, methane, or magma. The only advice I can give you is to be prepared.

Before you and your Master leave on any missions, you'll probably need to visit the quartermaster. In the quartermaster's office you can receive a supply of mission-specific gear to outfit you for whatever task has been assigned to you by the Council.

The most important thing to do on a mission is to follow the lead of your Master. You are a Padawan and you are still learning, but that doesn't mean you should not be ready. It's important to know your surroundings and your equipment. You should learn the strengths and weaknesses of your standard field equipment package.

The **A88 Aquata Breather** is rated for up to two hours of oxygen intake, but is easily calibrated for mixtures of different gases if you belong

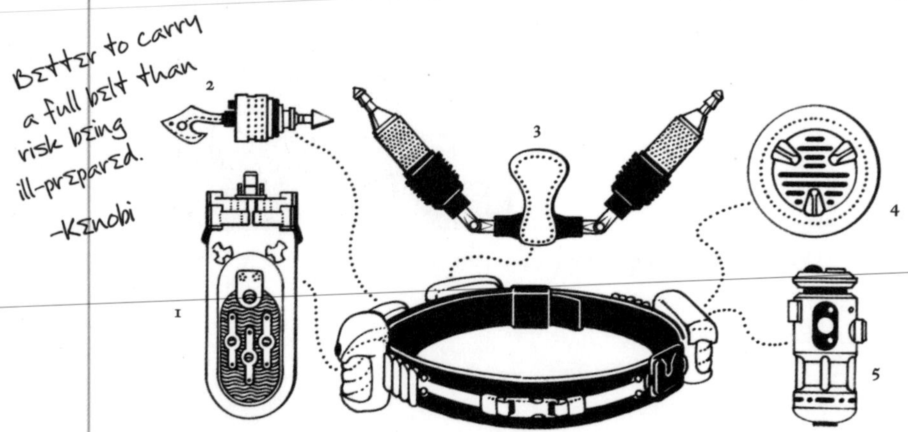
Better to carry a full belt than risk being ill-prepared.
-Kenobi
1
2
3
4
5

3-43 A standard field utility belt holds: 1. comlink; 2. grappling hook; 3. Aquata Breather; 4. imagecaster; 5. beacon transceiver.

to a species with specific respiratory needs. These breathers are most commonly used for underwater travel, but they can easily save your life in toxic or thin atmospheres.

The **Jedi beacon transceiver** should be kept with you at all times. It is a hyperwave device keyed to the Temple on a proprietary, signal-locked frequency. That means you can instantly communicate with the Temple from a range of up to 48,000 light-years, or with another Jedi's transceiver as long as the signal is bounced through the Temple first. In an emergency, this device will allow you to receive news from the Order.

The **compressed-air grappling hook** comes equipped with a liquid reservoir. When the hook is fired, the liquid hardens, turning into a high-tensile cable with a maximum length of 21 meters and a tested breaking point of 550 kilograms.

Hardly! It broke when we evacuated the Princess of Quanducial down the palace wall!
-Thame

The **comlink** is a Kultech KP-009. This is a durable model with a factory-guaranteed range of 100 kilometers to permit surface-to-orbit communications, and can also emit a shroud of white noise to block eavesdroppers. Use this to stay in touch with your Master if you are separated.

Also carry a smuggler's scrambler. Jedi signals are easily intercepted by slicers.
Q-G

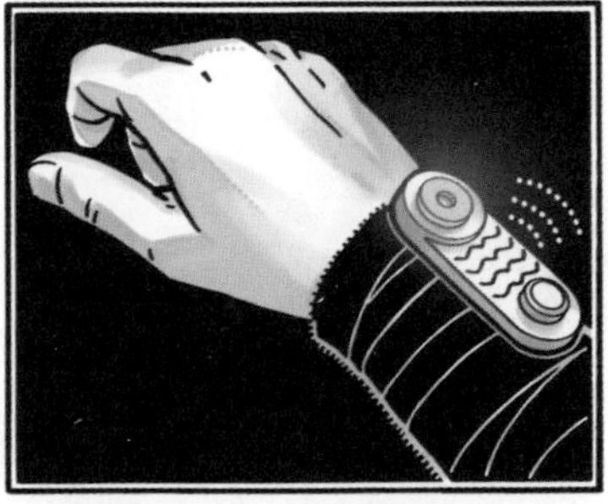

3.44 A WRIST COMLINK ALLOWS JEDI TO COMMUNICATE WHILE KEEPING THEIR HANDS FREE.

The **imagecaster**, a Soronsian Holox mark Null, projects holomaps or other 3-D images. This includes holographic communications when used in conjunction with your beacon transceiver.

Other items, including nutrient capsules, a glow rod, and lightsaber repair tools, are standard issue equipment in any field kit. These items can be found in your utility belt.

WHY NOT JUST USE YOUR LIGHTSABER?
Anakin

Using the Temple's Analysis Chamber

I've at times worked as a Jedi investigator and have gained experience among regular people, which led me to confront a disagreeable truth—the Force is limited in its applications. A talented Jedi can detect the emotional residue from an object and even perceive flashes of past events, but sometimes the Force fails you. In those instances you should feel no shame in turning over your investigation to one of our JN-66 analysis droids.

AGREED. UNLIKE SOME JEDI, I'VE NO OBJECTION TO WORKING WITH DROIDS.
—DOOKU

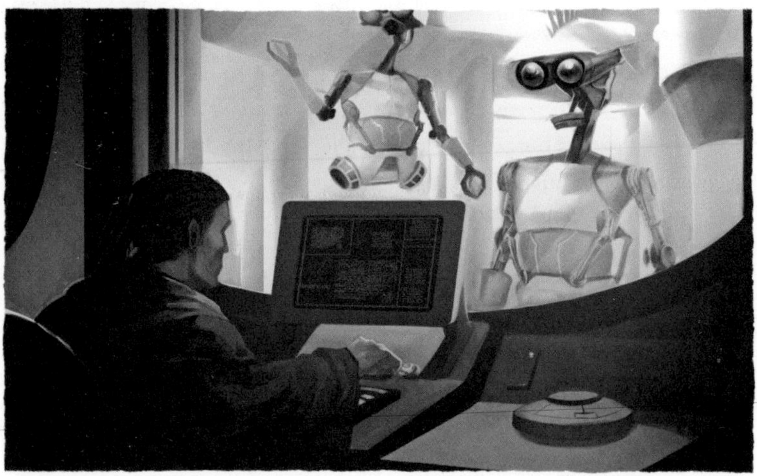

3.45 Input screens let a Jedi interact with the droids in the vacuum chamber.

The Temple's Analysis Chamber is on level Alek-5 in the First Knowledge Quarter. This facility is equipped for full spectral and molecular analysis of artifacts and data recordings. Don't let an over-reliance on Jedi training prevent you from using this resource once in a while.

The chamber has several Cybot Galactica JN-66 units along with a handful of SP-4 models to tackle the more menial duties. The facility is, by necessity, entirely sterile. The laboratory is scoured of all micro-organisms that might taint the proceedings and in many cases is kept at full vacuum. Anything you wish to

Remember to be specific or the droids may blow a fuse. -Thame

drop off for scanning by the droids should be left in the receiving slot, along with a summary of what you hope to uncover, an overview of the object, and an explanation of how it came into your possession.

From experience, I recommend that you simply state the desired outcome of the analysis, *not* the specific scans needed to determine that outcome. The equipment in this facility can create a holo-image of a single atomic bond, so very little can escape its attention. Any given sample may be subject to—at least—thermal, microoptic, electromagnetic, chemical, sonic, and radiation testing.

The chamber's computers are linked to both the Jedi Archives and the Galactic City Police central database, so any criminal evidence is likely to find a match as soon as the analysis has run its course. It's up to us Jedi to gather the data, but the droids are programmed to take it from there.

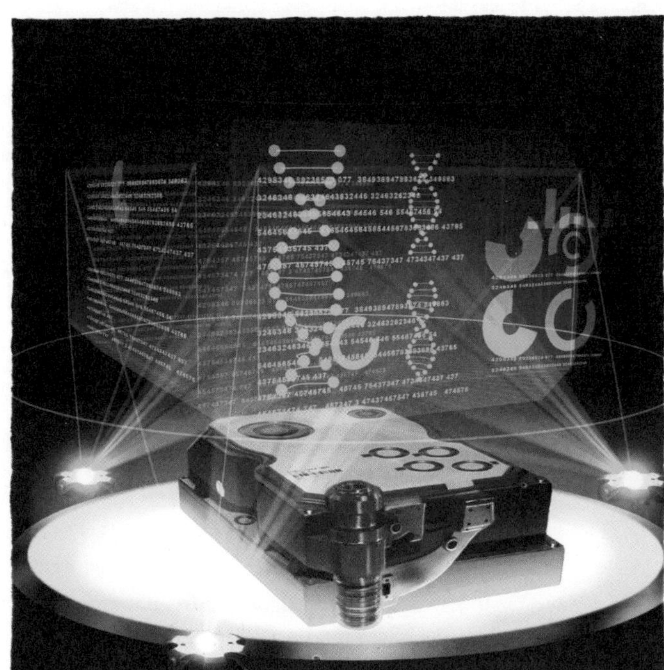

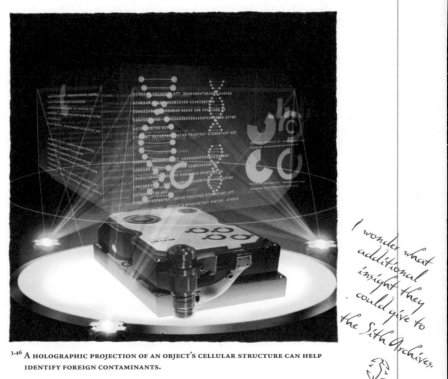

3.46 A HOLOGRAPHIC PROJECTION OF AN OBJECT'S CELLULAR STRUCTURE CAN HELP IDENTIFY FOREIGN CONTAMINANTS.

I wonder what additional insight they could give to the Sith Archives.

Advanced Cultures and Politics in the Republic

By Bowspritz, Jedi Biologist

Once you leave the Temple on a mission, the variety and complexity of life outside Coruscant becomes inescapable. For reasons both biological and cultural, many species play specialized roles in interstellar relations. What follows is a partial list of those influential cultural players, but it's a good idea to dive in and interact with them firsthand.

OR THE RANKS OF BOUNTY HUNTERS! -AHSOKA

3.47 Duros

- **Duros** are among the galaxy's oldest space travelers. Originating on the Core World of Duro, they are in fact rarely found there. Instead they dominate the ranks of for-hire pilots and the staffs of busy space stations. In my experience a Duros always has a story to tell, but it helps if you buy a round of Gizer ales first.

3.48 Bith

- The **Biths** of Clak'dor VII are mathematicians. They're also outstanding musicians, which to them is really just another way of saying the same thing. Biths perceive musical tones as easily as other species see colors, so don't miss a chance to take in a live performance.

3.49 Herglic

- **Herglics** have been in the business of interstellar trade for over 27,000 years. The Jedi Temple is one of many Coruscant entities that employs Herglics for the import and export of contracts.

- Humans dominate much of the politics here on Coruscant, but **Corellians** are a unique and memorable human breed. Brave, cocky, and charismatic, they consider themselves better pilots than any Duros could ever hope to be. YES, THIS SOUNDS LIKE HAN. WEDGE TOO. -LUKE

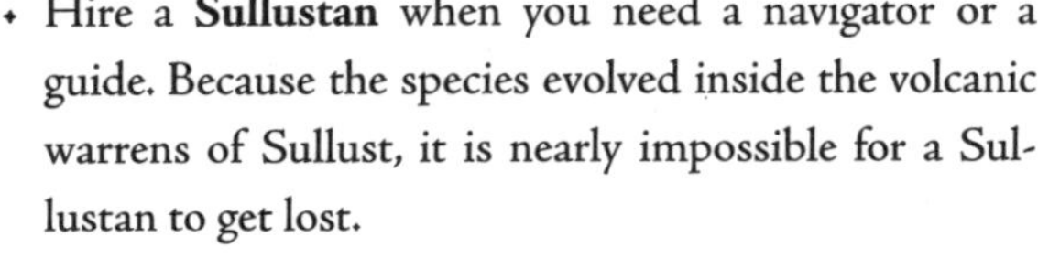

- Hire a **Sullustan** when you need a navigator or a guide. Because the species evolved inside the volcanic warrens of Sullust, it is nearly impossible for a Sullustan to get lost.

3.50 Sullustan

- **Hutts**, of course, rule Hutt Space—the galaxy's largest political power other than the Republic now that the war with the Sith is over. Hutts are brilliant strategists who often think five moves ahead, so don't underestimate them.

- **Bothans** are in charge of Bothan Space, a small enclave centered on Bothawui in the Mid Rim. Because the territory is politically neutral, it is a haven for spies from a thousand different factions.

3.51 Bothan

- **Squibs** are among the galaxy's greatest scavengers. Though they have a reputation as thieves, Squibs are shrewd judges of value and can fix machines that appear hopelessly damaged. Squibs have got me out of more than a few jams, though the experiences did some damage to my credit line with the Temple.

3.52 Squib

They are thieves! Why Master Qui-Gon thinks it's okay to let them pocket my focusing crystal I can't imagine.

-Kenobi

THEY'RE BATTLEFIELD SCAVENGERS TOO—GOOD SOURCE OF DATA ON SEP MOVEMENTS.

-AHSOKA

Aliens Resistant to Force Abilities

My specialty is alien biology, and as a Jedi I recognize that the fundamental unifier of all life is the Force. It is fascinating how the Force inspires such a variety of change and adaptation, even allowing species to develop barriers that redirect the Force's natural flow. Because such evolutions can be found among recognized sentient beings, you should be able to identify these species on sight if you wish to use your Jedi abilities to their fullest.

3.53 Hutt

Hutts You and your Master will probably run across a Hutt's thugs long before you meet an actual Hutt, but don't use mind tricks if you're brought before their boss! Hutts are notoriously difficult to influence or read through the Force. Their elusiveness has been a struggle for the Jedi since our forebears left Tython.

AND I THOUGHT IT WAS JUST JABBA! -LUKE

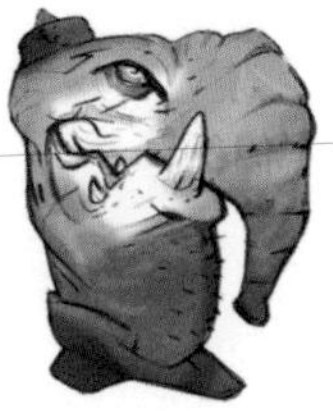

3.54 Toydarian

Toydarians These fascinating beings have lighter-than-air gases in their bellies that enable flight in standard or less-than-standard gravities. But remember that Toydarians are resistant to mind tricks, illusions, and telepathic suggestions. They are well aware of this fact and boast that they can easily outsmart a Jedi. Do not haggle with a Toydarian vendor!

Must have Pestage find some to assist my Jedi hunters.

3.55 Dashade

Dashade This species nearly vanished after the supernova destruction of their homeworld, but a few survivors remain, including Snar Extruct, who works with Master Vaunk as her sparring partner. Dashade are resistant to all direct applications of the Force, including telekinetic shoves and pulls, and they cannot be sensed by a Jedi even when standing at arm's length. It is a tragedy that the Sith recruited so many Dashade as assassins during the last war and reduced their numbers even further.

3.56 Yinchorri

Yinchorri These reptilians are immune to mental manipulation and cannot have their internal balance disrupted by advanced Force techniques. Their warriors also wear cortosis armor, so don't pick a fight.

They're still making trouble. And they killed Master Giiett. -Kenobi

SOME HAVE NOW JOINED CRIME CARTELS. THEY'RE TOUGH. Anakin

3.57 B'rknaa

B'rknaa Like most rock-based creatures, this species from the moon Indobok can be particularly inscrutable since their microscopic structures are so different from midi-chlorian-infused organic cells. All B'rknaa share a communal mind and are resistant to every direct Force application.

THEY'VE JOINED SOME PIRATE CREWS TOO— WE CAN TAKE THEM! -AHSOKA

3.58 Shi'ido

Shi'ido and **Polydroxol** Both species are shapeshifters. Don't underestimate them. Due to their fluid structures, getting a fix on a shapeshifter in the Force can feel like grabbing a fleek eel. The Shi'ido and the liquid-metal Polydroxol are among the most enigmatic species I have ever encountered in my research.

Force-Wielding Animals

Why *shouldn't* animals use the Force? That was my thought when I first heard of the phenomenon as an Initiate, before I started down the path that ultimately gave me the honorific of beastmaster. Since that time I've seen plenty of evidence that the Force can be an evolutionary advantage, just like spines or antlers.

3.59 Vornskr

Central to any such discussions are the vornskrs and ysalamiri of a classified world. Their abilities caused the Council to quarantine the entire system. **Vornskrs** are quadrupedal predators that can sense the Force and can use that sense to home in on their prey. So because Jedi are strong in the Force, they appear as the biggest and tastiest meal a vornskr has ever encountered. Beware the enemy that utilizes this ability to hunt Jedi.

Though vornskrs are organic "Jedi detectors," their Force abilities are negligible compared to those of the **ysalamiri**—arboreal lizards that create bubbles or voids in the Force that hide their energy from predators like vornskrs. Enough ysalamiri clustered together can generate a void large enough to disable an army of Jedi from using the Force.

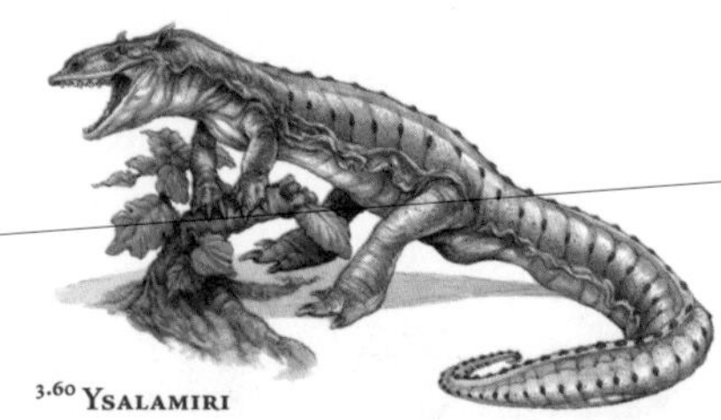

3.60 Ysalamiri

IF THE JEDI HAD BEEN LESS SECRETIVE ABOUT MYRKR, I WOULDN'T HAVE BEEN SO SURPRISED BY WHAT I FOUND THERE.
–LUKE

Equally dangerous are the **taozin,** annelids the size of hovertrains found on the moon of Va'art. The nodules on a taozin carapace interfere with a Jedi's Sense abilities, making the taozin appear invisible in the Force. This also applies to those who carry taozin nodules.

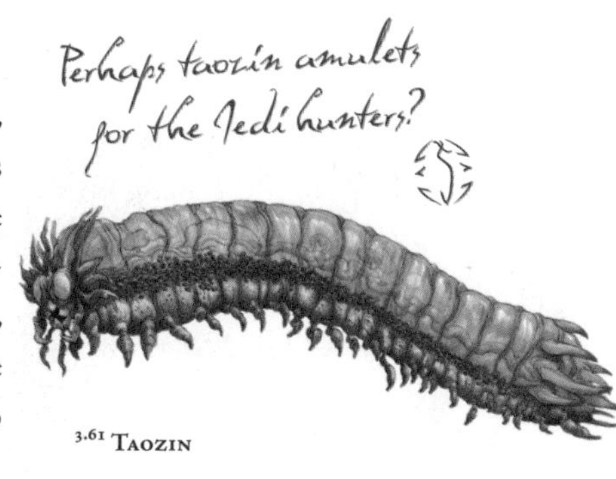

Perhaps taozin amulets
for the Jedi hunters?

3.61 Taozin

WOULDN'T WANT TO MEET
ONE OF THESE IN THE DARK!
-AHSOKA

3.62 Nighthunter

Also among dangerous predators that use the Force are **nighthunters,** which have more in common with taozin than vornskrs. They can manipulate the Force to create a cloak of shadows around themselves. Because nighthunters are sometimes used as guard beasts, it would be beneficial for you to learn to recognize their silhouettes.

Other Force-sensitive animals are more benign. **Beck-tori** are aquatic parasites from Nam Priax, but they can be found on many temperate ocean worlds. These creatures use the Force to enhance their senses to locate prey. They have also been known to use the Force to help heal their injuries.

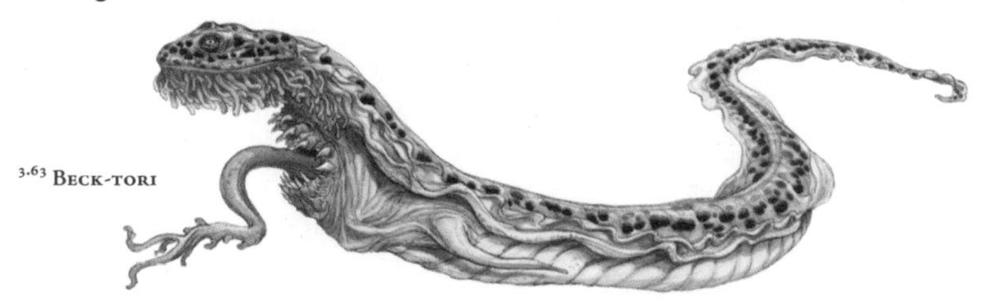

3.63 Beck-tori

I've heard their hides are resistant to sabers as well.
-Kenobi

3.64 Akk dog

Akk dogs are commonly seen as Jedi pets or companions. I first encountered these animals on Ord Canfre's ExplorCorps outpost, but didn't think there was anything unusual about the bond they shared with their trainers. I soon discovered, however, that akk dogs will form a Force bond with any handler—Jedi or not—through an empathic link heightened by a degree of rudimentary telepathy.

Jakobeasts are my favorite example of a Force adaptation. These arctic herd animals can use their horns to generate a telekinetic push. A herd of them can create a wave strong enough to flatten forests.

This is the truth! Flipped our speeder too!
-Thame

These animals are but a few of the known creatures with the ability to use the Force. As you travel outside the Temple, keep your mind and your eyes open and never underestimate your fellow creatures in the Force.

3.65 Jakobeast

Studying Aboard Praxeum Ships

A tremendous Opportunity to expand one's knowledge of the Living Force.
Q-G

By Crix Sunburris, Jedi Ace

The Exploration Corps is the branch of the Jedi Service Corps I most respect because it never stops pushing boundaries. The ExplorCorps seeks my advice whenever possible, and one practice I continue to champion is the use of praxeum ships.

These interstellar vessels are operated and crewed by members of the ExplorCorps, but they play host to Initiates, Padawans, Knights, and even honored Jedi Masters such as myself. They range in size from converted cargo freighters up to custom-built Corellian Colonizers that are more than three hundred meters long.

These Corellian ships are the pride of the ExplorCorps. There are three in service—the *Beneficia*, the *Luminosity*, and the *Silikan Stillness*. At one point the Order operated as many as thirteen, but most didn't survive the recent war with the Sith. These three vessels regularly patrol the Core, the Rim, and fringes of Wild Space.

If you're called aboard a praxeum ship, consider yourself lucky! As a Padawan I would have given anything to share my knowledge with the Jedi working in galactic trouble spots. Most of your time aboard these vessels will be spent training, including lightsaber sparring and studying languages and cultures. The ships can accommodate more than a thousand Jedi each, and have facilities including meditation chambers, libraries, gymnasiums, starfield holomaps, and medical wings.

"BOOKBARGES" IS WHAT PADAWANS USED TO CALL THEM.
-AHSOKA

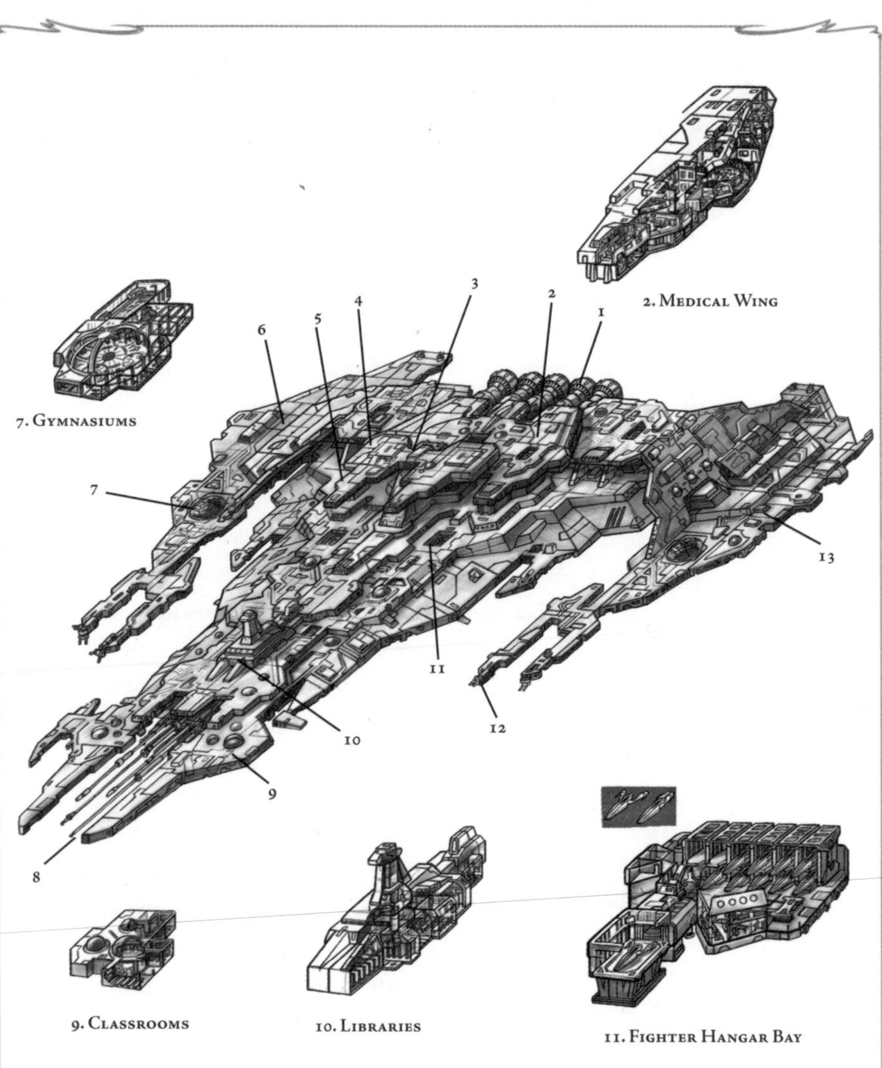

3.66 Corellian Colonizer ship:

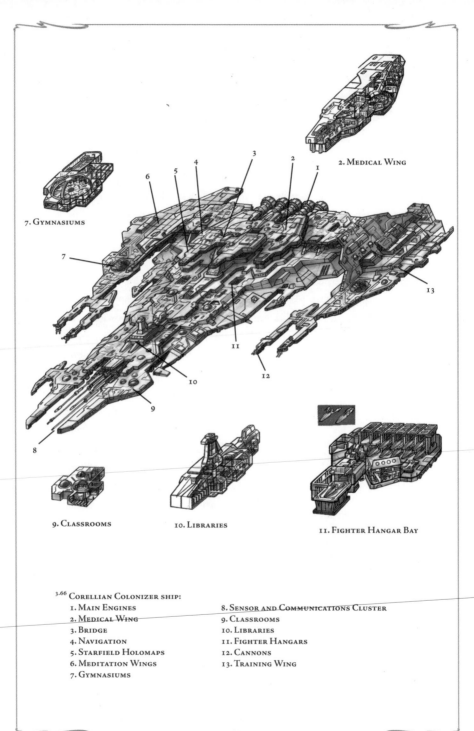

1. Main Engines
2. Medical Wing
3. Bridge
4. Navigation
5. Starfield Holomaps
6. Meditation Wings
7. Gymnasiums
8. Sensor and Communications Cluster
9. Classrooms
10. Libraries
11. Fighter Hangars
12. Cannons
13. Training Wing

At any moment a Jedi praxeum ship can be called upon to assist after a planetary disaster or to intervene in a civil war. Consequently the ships carry laser and ion cannons (installed during the war) and have hangars for lightweight starfighters.

With the defeat of the Sith, more resources can now be focused on projects like praxeum ships. One proposal I'm personally advancing is the construction of a new, peacetime praxeum at the Abhean Shipyards. It will be called the *Sunburris* and will stretch two kilometers long and one kilometer wide. It will be a sight to behold.

Took shape this vessel did many centuries later as the Chu'unthor. Still lost to the witches it is.
—Yoda

DECIDED NOT TO RAISE THE CHU'UNTHOR FROM ITS CRASH SITE. IT WILL REMAIN A MEMORIAL.
—LUKE

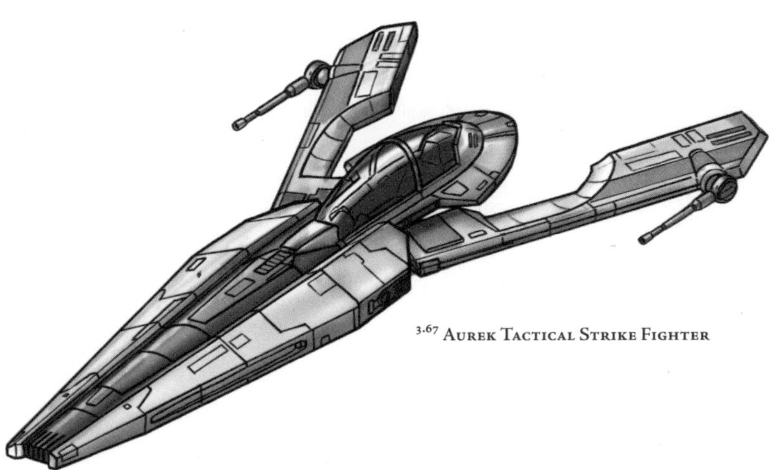

3.67 AUREK TACTICAL STRIKE FIGHTER

THE JEDI TRIALS

BY RESTELLY QUIST, CHIEF LIBRARIAN

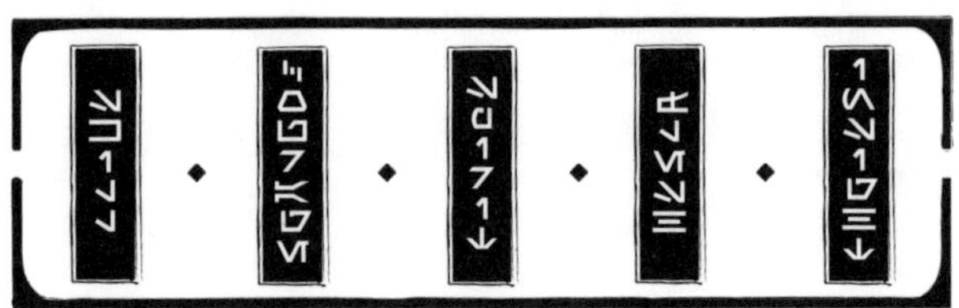

Your apprenticeship is a temporary thing. At some point you will have learned all you can from your Master, and one-on-one study will no longer benefit either of you. When that day comes, you must be prepared for the Jedi trials.

MASTER OBI-WAN DIDN'T HAVE TO PASS THE FORMAL TRIALS, SO I DON'T SEE WHY I SHOULD. Anakin

The Trials of Knighthood date back to the birth of the Order on Tython during the pre-Republic era. For thousands of years, they had no fixed structure and instead centered on the assessment of individual Masters regarding the fitness of their students. While the Council encourages a strong bond between Master and Padawan, the flaws in this arrangement were clear: Masters can develop inflated opinions of their students due to shared experiences, or conversely can become their students' worst critics in an effort to improve them.

EVER SINCE THE START OF THE WAR, IT'S LIKE EVERYBODY'S FORGOTTEN ABOUT THE TRADITIONAL TRIALS. -AHSOKA

Neutral, dispassionate judgment and objective standards provide more verifiable benchmarks from which to judge the skill of a Padawan. The current battery of Jedi trials—instated after the relaxed standards of the last war—consists of five challenges:

- **Trial of Skill** Demonstrates a Jedi's competence with a lightsaber and the Force principles of Control.
- **Trial of Courage** Establishes a Jedi's skill and fortitude in the face of danger and overwhelming odds.
- **Trial of Spirit** Tests a Jedi's ability to vanquish inner battles and emerge unscathed.

- **Trial of the Flesh** Determines a Jedi's capacity to overcome great pain.
- **Trial of Insight** Reveals a Jedi's aptitude for distinguishing reality from illusion through deceptive challenges.

Sounds tricky! —Thame

Your examination will take place in the Jedi trials Chamber unless the Council has made other arrangements.

Trial of Skill

Don't be fooled into thinking of the Trial of Skill as a physical challenge. Master Vaunk and the Council members will judge your performance based on a series of lightsaber tests, but in truth this Trial hinges on a Jedi's ability to maintain self-discipline in the face of distraction.

Lightsaber combat is attached to the Trial of Skill as a matter of modern convenience, for every Jedi must demonstrate the ability to wield a blade. Yet lightsaber combat springs from the discipline of Control. Early in the history of the Order, the Trial of Skill took many forms, including acrobatics while balanced on the tip of a wooden staff and keeping a single pebble suspended while standing in the vortex of a howling Tythonese hailstorm.

3.68 The Trial of Skill is not a test of athleticism, but of control.

Difficult this is, for those who lack focus. —Yoda

Do not bother to anticipate what type of lightsaber challenge you will encounter during the Trial of Skill or which opponent you will face. The popular rumor among Padawans is that you must outlast the Jedi Battlemaster in a session that may span hours. This *could* be true, for aching fatigue provides exactly the kind of challenge to a Jedi's focus that the Trial of Skill

[3.69] Through tangible holoprojectors, Padawans might test their skills against a Sith Lord.

is meant to evaluate. Yet you may face multiple opponents at once; a succession of fresh opponents while you become increasingly exhausted; a duel with one Jedi while another manipulates your perceptions or shifts the floor tiles beneath your feet; or perhaps even a duel with a member of the Council, including our venerable Grand Master—a rare privilege indeed.

Not fair! This is why Rouggle failed the trials! -Thame

Such challenges are not meant to be unfair. All are designed to mimic challenges you may one day face if you are to serve the Order and the Republic as a Jedi Knight.

The latest feature in the Jedi trials Chamber is a holographic projector, introduced after the victory at Ruusan and capable of creating enemies from the air itself. With this tool you might face Darth Ruin, Lord Kaan, or any of the worst monsters to ever rise from the dark side.

IN LIGHT OF THE JACEN AND TENEL KA ACCIDENT, I MAY HAVE PUSHED MY STUDENTS TO DEMONSTRATE THEIR LIGHTSABER SKILLS TOO SOON.

-LUKE

Trial of Courage

Even if your talents lean more toward diplomacy than war, courage is an intrinsic part of being a Jedi. Though the Force is with us, we are small in number when compared to the people of the galaxy. We have numerous enemies, and must also contend with those who do not understand our Order and therefore misinterpret our motives. As Jedi, we can never relax our discipline—nor can we fail to confront evil. A Jedi who is afraid to confront injustice is no Jedi at all, which makes the Trial of Courage a revelatory test.

I cannot tell you what you will face in your Trial of Courage. Its purpose is for a Padawan to persist in the face of fear. If you know what the trial will consist of, then the true measure of your courage will not be tested.

MASTER OBI-WAN PASSED THIS BY KILLING THE SITH ON NABOO. I'M GOING TO KILL THE SECOND SITH. Anakin

In previous eras, a Padawan was considered to have passed the Trial of Courage if he or she demonstrated battlefield heroics such as standing up to a vastly powerful Sith Lord. Similar dispensations were handed out by the Council during the last war. But in such situations it was at times difficult to sort out courage from recklessness. Overconfidence

And so you did, my predictable, manipulated apprentice.

3.70 The Trial of Courage measures a Padawan's willingness to fight evil despite the fear it may instill.

is a flaw, and rushing in unprepared can often make things worse. Courage must be aligned with the fourth precept of the Jedi Code: *There is no chaos, there is harmony.*

The war is over, but the Council may still assign special missions to Padawans who wish to pass the Trial of Courage. The mission could simply be a creation of the Council to test your reactions within the Jedi trials Chamber, or it could be deadly dangerous. Regardless of the nature of your challenge, it is important you do not share the details of your experience with your fellow Padawans. All must experience this Trial untainted.

Trial of the Flesh

For many Padawans, the Trial of the Flesh is the most difficult of the Knighthood trials. This ordeal will test your ability to overcome great pain, and it may be quite literal.

As a historian, I have studied the Trial of the Flesh in its incarnations throughout the millennia. During the Pius Dea era, the Jedi Order subjected Padawans to torments of cold, cuts, sonic shocks, and the application of sustained, low-powered blaster fire in the technique that the smugglers call "the Burning." Now condemned as barbarism, this practice is best understood as a product of its time. It did, however, crystallize the Trial of the Flesh's most fundamental principle: divorcing the self from the spirit.

During the most recent war against the Sith, the Council viewed battle as a living expression of the Trial of the Flesh. All Padawans who survived a war injury passed this Trial on the evidence of their scars. Padawans who had defeated a Sith Lord sometimes passed the Trials of the Flesh, Skill, and Courage simultaneously. Far from being a matter of political expediency, these battlefield trials have a long precedent in the Jedi Order. Padawans who lost a limb to *cho mok* or another Mark of Contact surrendered their flesh to demonstrate their commitment to the Jedi Order.

They reinstated this during the Arkanian Revolution. It's how Squire Kinning got her cyborg arm.
-Kenobi

I WANT TO BE A KNIGHT, BUT NOT THAT WAY!
-AHSOKA

It is now a different time, and we do not expect Padawans to prove their worth through wounds. The Trial of the Flesh, in fact, is about more than physical agony. The pain of loss is part of your passage from Padawan to Knight, for you are giving up the closest bond you have ever known. As the partnership with your Master is formally

QUI-GON WOULD HAVE BEEN MY MASTER. I'VE ALREADY LOST HIM—AND IT STILL FEELS TERRIBLE.
Anakin

3.71 Physical pain is one type of test a Padawan may face in the Trial of the Flesh.

[3.72] Emotional pain is another type of test one may face in the Trial of the Flesh.

dissolved, you may be overwhelmed by feelings of sadness or regret. This is part of your Trial of the Flesh. Think well on the first precept of the Jedi Code: *There is no emotion, there is peace.*

EMOTIONS DON'T NEED TO BE BANISHED, ONLY CONTROLLED I'VE DONE IT. Anakin

Trial of Spirit

Outsiders think that the Jedi exist to crusade against enemies—that we are mere counterbalances to the threat of the Sith. Only among our own ranks do we recognize that being a Jedi is an emotional commitment to a higher spirituality. This is the challenge represented by the Trial of Spirit, known among some as Facing the Mirror.

NOT AS WELL AS HE THINKS! -AHSOKA

Jedi possess great power, and those who have fallen to the dark side have unleashed their power in waves of misery. The Trial of Spirit measures your temptations and whether you can put them aside in the service of a greater cause. Although this is just as much a battle as the Trial of Skill, during this challenge you might not flex a single muscle. The battlescape is in your mind, and victory is marked by a profound sense of peace.

YODA WARNED ME BEFORE I ENTERED THE CAVE ON DAGOBAH, BUT I THOUGHT I COULD HANDLE ANYTHING. -LUKE

It is impossible to describe the Trial of Spirit. I do not know the fears coiled in your heart. Not even Grand Master Fae would presume to dictate your challenges. The Trial of Spirit is to be carried out under deep meditation, with a Master who will nudge you onto the path that you least wish to tread.

Under meditation you may feel that you've been transported off Coruscant entirely. You may see the faces of colleagues who have long since passed into the Force. You will undoubtedly see things that disturb you, from enemies you have faced to the most horrific cacodemons in the Core's nightmarish mythology.

Remember the third precept of the Jedi Code: *There is no passion, there is serenity*. Stay true to the discipline of self-control, and keep in mind that you are but an agent of the Force. Once you accept that grief, shame, revenge, and all other emotions that center on the self have no hold on you, you will emerge victorious. If you do not, you will emerge broken and screaming. You should hope you do not fail the Trial of Spirit.

3.73 DURING THE TRIAL OF SPIRIT, JEDI MUST MENTALLY FACE THEIR DEEPEST FEARS.

TRIAL OF INSIGHT

Can Jedi be deceived? Of course, but only if we ignore the will of the Force or the information in our Archives. A Jedi who is deceived is no longer working for the cause of the light side. In extreme cases, a Jedi operating under delusions may become a danger to innocents.

The Trial of Insight guards against this threat. It was the last test to be formalized as part of the Trials of Knighthood, and rose to prominence after it became clear that the Trials were producing Jedi who were brave, competent, and could overcome temptation—but who could not see through the patter of a simple con artist.

Insight!? We Sith grew right under their noses.

Deception and misdirection are threats to the Jedi, and our enemies frequently use them against us. The Hutts have been the ruin of countless Jedi campaigns throughout history, not due to their martial prowess but through their trickery. The Trial of Insight tests a Padawan's ability to see through illusion and judge the person beneath, and to filter out distractions in search of the truth.

Lenient we have been, in enforcing this trial. Not on their eyes, Padawans should learn to rely.
—Yoda

Over the centuries many challenges have been employed to assess this ability in the Trial of Insight. These include locating a single grain of sand within a field of stones, determining the content

3.74 In order to gain Insight, Jedi must be able to find truth amidst deceit and trickery.

and meaning of a fragmentary text from scattered pieces, and solving any of the High Riddles of Dwartii—and no, researching the riddles in the Archives beforehand is not permitted.

The Trial of Insight may occur at a moment when you are not prepared for it, and may in fact be part of an unrelated challenge. I am reminded of three Padawans undergoing the eighth hour of the Trial of Skill. Through a perceptual trick all were made to believe they faced a horde of angry warriors. One battled on in the face of certain defeat and passed her Trial of Courage. The second perceived the illusory nature of the combatants and passed his Trial of Insight. The third bowed out of the trial, citing exhaustion, and failed to become a Knight.

I was right—tricky! —Thame

3.75 Insight may also be gained by seeing beyond what is physically in front of you, to what is real.

Exceptions to the Jedi Trials

The purpose of the Trials of Knighthood, the post-Ruusan reformations, and the very volume you hold in your hands is to formalize what has at times been a messy process of recognizing a Jedi's progress within the Force. Through the strains of war, plague, and economic collapse the Republic has endured over the last few centuries, Jedi standards have grown distressingly negligent. No longer are battlefield promotions the norm, and no longer are Knights and Masters permitted final say in whether their Padawans are ready to graduate from their apprenticeships.

LOOKS LIKE THIS HAS SLIPPED AGAIN DURING THIS CURRENT WAR.
-AHSOKA

3.76 A Padawan must make a case before the Council to be considered for an exemption from any of the trials.

Though I do not approve, there are cases in which a Padawan may become a Knight while bypassing some or all of the trials. The current structure of five Jedi trials is designed to produce Knights in whom the Council has entrusted its confidence. Thus the Council may, at its discretion, promote any Jedi for any reason, or refuse such a promotion if its judgment warrants it. No Padawan should lobby for special treatment. ~~You do not know~~ better than the Council. There can be no appeal or dispute.

Unusual circumstances under which a Padawan may bypass one or more of the formal trials include:

- **Trial of Skill** Padawans who have bested a battlemaster during sparring, or who have demonstrated blindfolded mastery of the saber training exercise Faalo's Cadences, may be judged sufficiently advanced in this area that standard testing is redundant.
- **Trial of Courage** A variety of special dispensations can be given for this trial, encompassing Padawans who have succeeded in a difficult mission or who have saved the lives of their Masters.
- **Trial of Spirit** Padawans shown to have mastered their own dark side may be judged to have passed this trial. (During the war, this included followers of the Sith army who turned to the light.)
- **Trial of the Flesh** Significant pain and loss is considered a worthy demonstration, such as Initiates who were recruited later in life and have experienced the pain of loss and quieted their feelings for the family of their birth.
- **Trial of Insight** If a Padawan has demonstrated wisdom beyond his or her years and training, this may count as a pass—particularly if he or she divined a solution that avoided violence.

Rampant during the Clone Wars. Overconfident Jedi are easily killed.

MUCH AS I HATE TO AGREE WITH PALPATINE ON ANYTHING, I NEARLY LOST MY LIFE ON CLOUD CITY TO OVERCONFIDENCE.
I LOST A STUDENT, TOO.
-LUKE

I helped broker peace with the colicoids by trading food. Wonder if it will count?
-Thame

YODA DIDN'T KNIGHT ME, SO I DIDN'T KNIGHT MY OWN STUDENTS. WILL WORK ON FORMALIZING THIS.

-LUKE

THE KNIGHTING CEREMONY

BY GRAND MASTER FAE COVEN

If you have passed the trials, you will know it at once—there is little point in keeping Padawans in the dark regarding their status. However, you will not bear the title of Knight until the completion of the Knighting Ceremony. Proper etiquette must be followed during this most ancient of rituals. Prepare yourself, and do not embarrass your Master by forgetting your role.

3.77 WITHIN THE TRANQUILITY SPIRE, PADAWANS MUST REFLECT ON THE PATH THEY HAVE TAKEN TO ARRIVE AT THIS POINT.

One day before the appointed date, report to the heart of the Temple. Here in the preparation chamber at the center of the sacred Tranquility Spire, you will spend a day and a night in meditation. You may be alone, or there may be many Padawans sharing the space with you. <u>Do not use this time for socialization</u>, but instead reflect upon your journey as a Jedi and prepare yourself for what the Force wills for your future.

Focused Padawans must be during this step, for their future they must sense. —Yoda

On the following day you will be summoned to the Hall of Knighthood—most likely alone, but possibly with one or more of your fellow Knights-to-be. The members of the High Council will be present, along with your Master and other Jedi who played key roles in your development. If the High Council members are offworld or inaccessible, members of the Reassignment, Reconciliation, or First Knowledge Councils may sit in as appropriate.

All members of the Council will ignite their lightsabers to illuminate the darkened chamber. As the Grand Master or ranking Jedi approaches you, kneel to hear the words offered on your behalf. Bow your head when the Master recites the following passage:

By the right of the Council, by the will of the Force, I dub thee Knight of the Republic.

AN HONORABLE AND SOLEMN CEREMONY, EVEN FOR THOSE BORN TO NOBILITY. -DOOKU

The Master will lower his or her blade to your shoulder and bring it up in a swift motion to cut loose your Padawan braid. If you are not of a species that grows the braid, the blade will be brought to both shoulders (or sides of the body) and raised in a sharp salute.

You are now a Jedi Knight.

WONDER IF THEY'LL CUT MY BEADS? -AHSOKA

3.78 With his or her blade, a Grand Master confers knighthood on a Padawan.

If You Fail the Trials

Failure at any of the trials is equal to failure at all of them. But even success at all the trials does not guarantee a promotion to Jedi Knight. The Council is the final authority in all matters relating to the Order, including the ranks of its members.

Typical arrogance.

3.79 The Reassignment Council may supply the answer for failed Padawans in need of direction.

There are many cases in which Jedi who passed the trials received a rejection when the Council did not sense the will of the Force in their future. In other cases the Council has promoted those with little aptitude for the trials, under the conviction that the Force still had much work to do in their future lives as Jedi Knights. All of this is to say, do not be overconfident. You cannot will your Knighthood into existence with words or deeds, and accepting your subservience to the Council is an act of humility central to our existence as public servants.

If you fail the trials—and if the Council does not forbid it—you may try again. You will undoubtedly wish to spend the intervening time in study and training. If your Master permits, you may even return to your familiar Padawan apprenticeship. However, this is a temporary arrangement, and you must select a date for your second round of trials.

There is nothing printed in any tome of Jedi regulations that limits how many times you may take the trials, but such determinations are made at the Council's indulgence. Repeated failures will not be tolerated, and are evidence that you are defying the Force's plan for your destiny. Accept that you will not become a Knight, and meditate on what the Force is saying. It is advised to spend up to several weeks without food or rest during this period of meditation as you purge your body and mind of distractions.

You can always continue your time with the Order in the Jedi Service Corps, or within the ranks of the Temple staff. You may retain the rank of Padawan if you choose, even though you are no longer a formal apprentice. You may also wish to go by the simple rank of "Jedi."

Half-Moonsing did this! He's the caretaker of the speeder pool.
–Thame

PERMITTING FAILURES TO REMAIN IN THE TEMPLE IS AN EXPRESSION OF PITY, NOTHING MORE. –DOOKU

Half-Moonsing is a Jedi of great insight, regardless of his station.
Q-G

Don't know who Half-Moonsing is, but I'm not about to mess with anyone in the speeder pool.
-Kenobi

PART 4

DARTH SIDIOUS

PART IV
JEDI KNIGHT

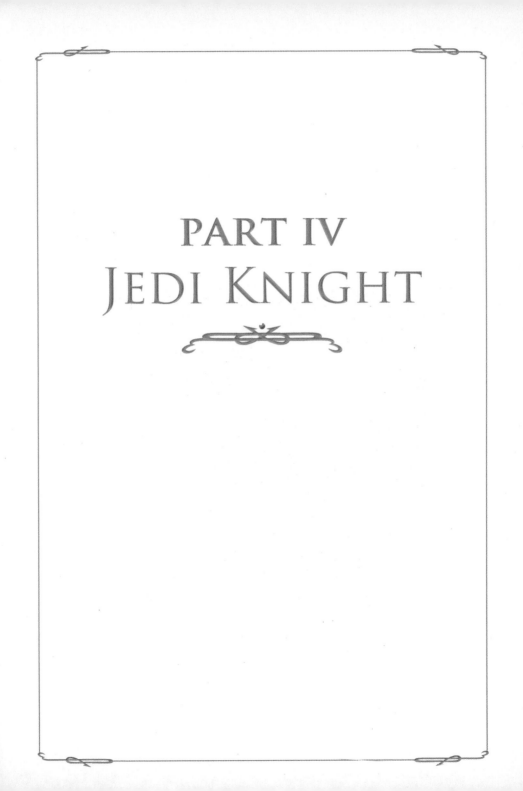

Roles and Duties of a Jedi Knight

By Grand Master Fae Coven

Upon your graduation to knighthood, you will be a full member of the Order in the eyes of all. As a Jedi Knight you will travel the galaxy and aid all those you encounter. You are no longer bound to a Master, and can thus choose your own approach to solving the dilemmas laid before you.

4.1 A Jedi Knight is always welcome on Coruscant, but they are citizens of the galaxy.

Of course, you will still be subject to the demands of the Council. The Council, or one of the proxies in our satellite academies, will determine the missions you execute. As a Jedi Knight you are the arms and legs of the Order, and the Council requires you to stay fit and

4.2 MANY SPECIES LOOK TO THE JEDI FOR IMPARTIAL JUDGMENT.

prepared for the moment when you will be asked to end threats to the citizens of the galaxy.

There are more Knights than any other rank of Jedi in the Order, and there are many paths Jedi Knights may follow in their careers. Knights perform several functions within the Order, including peacekeeping, diplomacy, and investigation. Such talent specialization has given rise to three distinct branches of Knights and Masters: Jedi Guardians, Jedi Consulars, and Jedi Sentinels. Each group differs greatly in its approach to carrying out a mission, but all three philosophies are vital to the Order. Allow the Force to guide you into a role that will best utilize your innate abilities.

Even more than younglings? -Thame

Your service as a Jedi Knight can last decades, even centuries if you belong to a species blessed with longevity. Throughout these years you will serve in the name of the Republic and at the will of the Force—an opportunity few beings will ever know.

Blessed I am. -Yoda

Guardian the title is, not Warrior. Remember this all Knights should.
—Yoda

Jedi Guardian

By Crix Sunburris, Jedi Ace

If you prefer heroics to standing around, becoming a Jedi Guardian may be the path for you. While I'm not here to disparage the work of our Jedi Consulars and Sentinels, it's a fact that we Guardians are the Republic's first line of defense against the thousand enemies who seek to destroy it.

AGREED. WHY BECOME A JEDI IF YOU DON'T FIGHT?
Anakin

LOOKS LIKE YOU GOT YOUR WISH—EVERYBODY'S A FIGHTER NOW.
-AHSOKA

The Guardians are the heirs of the first Jedi Knights. When the first faction of Tythonese left their homeworld, they did so with the express purpose of making the wild galactic frontier safe for innocents—and with the same principles we uphold today. It's primarily this branch of the Order that is identified with lightsabers. The lightsaber is our weapon and our symbol.

Once you choose to specialize as a Jedi Guardian, training will consume your offhours. Your time is no longer subject to the demands of a Master, so neglect of your exercises is at your own peril. Each day I set aside time for one hour of running, one hour of unarmed combat drills, and one hour of saber cadences or sparring.

4.3 Most Jedi Guardians carry a blue lightsaber to show solidarity.

Although the Sith were extinguished in the last war, the current reality of peacetime has only heightened the importance of the Guardians. Following the postwar governmental reformations, the Republic no longer has a standing military. We are essentially the Republic's army, and must be ready to give up our lives in the service of this cause.

In a sense we are also the Republic's police force, responsible for keeping the peace and detaining lawbreakers. The services of Guardians are in desperate need among the worlds of the Outer Rim and Wild Space, where local security forces hold little sway and the people are in need of saviors.

This arrogance was what earned Jedi the people's hatred.

Jedi Guardians usually carry blue-bladed lightsabers, though doing so is more a sign of fraternity than a mandate. You can use whatever blade you're comfortable with, though I am certain you will wish to replace your original apprentice saber. We're warriors, so your lightsaber will see plenty of use! With enough heroics, you may one day join me and earn the honorific of Warrior Master.

4-4 JEDI GUARDIANS SERVE TO PROTECT GALACTIC PEACE AND AS SUCH SHOULD ALWAYS CARRY A SET OF WRIST BINDERS.

There are many paths to follow within the ranks of the Jedi Guardians. The ways of war are numerous, and no single Jedi can be the best at them all.

Jedi Peacekeepers

The Jedi Peacekeepers specialize in security and policing, and are among the oldest groups recognized by the Order. Though all of them are fine warriors, they do not normally serve as frontline combat troops and are instead trained in crowd control, apprehending suspects and shutting down threats before things can turn violent. At the request of planetary governors, peacekeepers are stationed on Republic worlds, where they work as liaisons to local law enforcement and militias.

Temple Security

On Coruscant, Peacekeepers are synonymous with Temple Security. These Jedi watch over the Jedi Temple and the surrounding district, keeping the area safe from eccentrics, zealots, and armed radicals. The ranks of Temple Security include Jedi Gatekeepers, who monitor the main entrance, and Jedi Brutes, whose imposing bulk often scares away troublemakers.

LIKE OLD JUROKK—HE'LL BE STUCK IN THAT JOB FOREVER.
Anakin

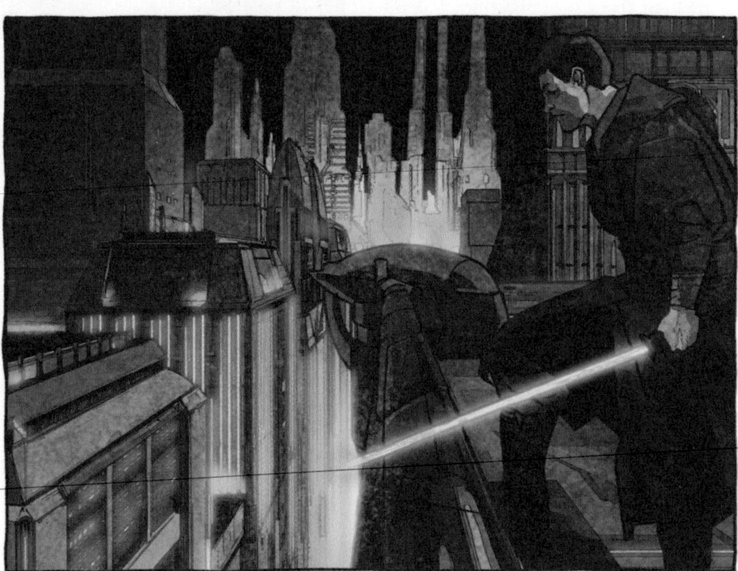

4.5 Jedi Snipers stand guard atop the Temple to keep watch over the city.

WONDER IF I WOULD HAVE SERVED HERE HAD I BEEN BORN IN ANOTHER ERA?
—LUKE

JEDI STARFIGHTERS

Members of the Jedi Starfighter Corps, known as Jedi Aces, pilot a fleet of Savage Star fighters, our starfighter of choice over the somewhat outdated Kuat Redshift we used to beat the Sith. These ships are equipped with twin laser cannons, a Chempat deflector shield, and an external hyperdrive sled.

CAN'T WAIT TO GET MY HANDS ON A TEMPLE STARFIGHTER!
Anakin

4.6 THE SAVAGE STAR

Jedi Aces use the Force to enhance reaction speed, targeting precision and battle awareness, but we never use it to cloud the perceptions of our enemies. We're Aces, and shortcuts of that kind are not needed.

As Jedi Aces, we travel all across the galaxy, sometimes hitching rides aboard Republic capital ships. During the war these were Republic Navy vessels. After the reformations, of course, the Navy no longer exists, but Aces are welcomed by all sector and planetary defense forces.

I've served with the Aces for nearly twenty years. In that time I've upgraded our fighter squadrons, destroyed more than 300 enemy craft, and earned the honorary title Air Marshal of the Republic. Don't be intimidated by these achievements—no one in the Starfighter Corps expects you to reach such heights. But we do need good pilots!

LOVE IT! THAT'S ME AFTER THE WAR—JEDI ACE.
—AHSOKA

LIGHTSABER INSTRUCTORS

Lightsabers are integral to our identity as an Order. As soon as Initiates are old enough to stand, they are instructed in the proper handling of a saber, and this instruction never truly ends until a Jedi has become one with the Force.

WHY WON'T MASTER DRALLIG LET ME STUDY THIS? IT'S NOT LIKE I'M GOING TO LEARN IT FROM OBI-WAN. *Anakin*

It should therefore be evident that lightsaber instructors are among the most vital players in the Jedi Order. If this lifestyle sounds interesting to you, slow down! This is not a specialization you take on without first proving your mettle in combat. Unlike the Consulars, we Guardians don't put much faith in teachers-for-life, and saber instructors bear the scars that attest to hundreds of combat kills. While it's true that the Jedi Order avoids violence wherever possible, it is at times necessary. In that light, who has the abilities best suited for a combat instructor—a diplomat or a warrior?

The Temple has one instructor who bears the title of battlemaster, currently Master Vaunk. The battlemaster designation was once held by only a single Jedi at a time, but the title grew in popularity during the war until it encompassed hundreds of generals and Jedi Lords. Most of these now serve at satellite Jedi academies and aboard praxeum ships. Battlemasters train Initiates and Padawans in the use of Forms I through VI combat moves and cadences, and impart knowledge about Form VII to those who have earned their trust.

THEY TAKE ON TOO MUCH. SOMEONE WHO SPENT ALL HIS TIME STUDYING A SINGLE FORM COULD PROBABLY BEST A BATTLEMASTER. —DOOKU

Beneath the battlemasters, day-to-day instructors serve to reinforce the proper execution of these styles. All lightsaber instructors are Jedi Masters, and must be recommended by a battlemaster and ratified by the High Council.

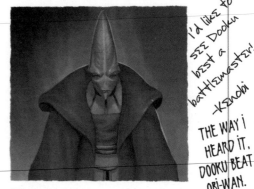

4.7 MASTER VAUNK

I'd like to see Dooku best a battlemaster! —Kenobi

THE WAY I HEARD IT, DOOKU BEAT OBI-WAN. —AHSOKA

The position of lightsaber instructor is one that Jedi Masters may achieve toward the end of their careers, when their reflexes have slowed but their minds are still sharp. It can also be a role filled by the preternaturally gifted, who possess skill with a saber running so deep it is foolish to waste them on Rim patrol.

4.8 The High Council is responsible for conferring the title of battlemaster.

Exotic Weapons Specialists

Although the lightsaber is our primary weapon, it is not the only type of armament available to the Jedi. The starfighter, for example, is a specialized weapon used by Jedi Aces, but there are many other tools used by those in the Order to fulfill specific missions or to exploit unique skill sets. Exotic Weapons Specialists are rare within the ranks of the Jedi Guardians, but they are respected for their mastery of difficult and esoteric disciplines. Mastery of any of the following weapons could earn you the title of Exotic Weapons Specialist:

- The **double-bladed lightsaber** and **lightsaber pike** are lightsaber variants that require combat specialization. These experts sometimes wield quarterstaffs with no energy blades at all. These can be made of lightsaber-resistant metal, or can be humble wooden staffs strengthened through the Force.

Thought these were only training devices for learning to wield a double-blade . . . —Thame

4.9 A Force-strengthened quarterstaff can resist lightsaber strikes.

- **Whips** can be made of leather, wire, cord, or energy tendrils—as in the lightwhip. Experts with whips use them to ensnare arms and legs, allowing them to disarm enemies or force them to the floor.

- **Flails** are a class of weapon using a weighted ball attached to a handle by means of a rope or chain. They are difficult weapons to master, but an expert in flails can use the ball to crack bones, the chain to entangle, and the handle—which is often adorned with a blade—to injure at close range.

We ran into three assassins with chain-sickles on Filve. Barely made it out of that alive. —Thame

I've tried to use one. Tangles easily. Q-G

WHY BOTHER? A LIGHTSABER CUTS THROUGH CHAINS. Anakin

[4.10] Flails have multiple uses but require intense combat training.

- **Ranged weapons** are not often employed by the Jedi, but there is no inherent shame in striking from a distance—though you will have to endure the curiosity of your peers. Jedi who have trained in blaster rifles as their specialization use the Force to enhance their vision and guide their shots. Most of the Temple's snipers use their lightsabers as ranged weapons, throwing them with distance and precision to take out targets.

So uncivilized. -Kenobi

- Some Jedi use their bodies as weapons. The **martial artists** of Bakuuni Hand employ the Force to strengthen their hands, feet, and forearms when making an unarmed strike. A blow from a Bakuuni master can pulverize stone.

Most Exotic Weapons Specialists devote their lives to the mastery of their chosen subject. Like lightsaber combat instructors, they often enter a teaching phase after they have achieved the rank of Master.

JEDI CONSULAR

BY SABLA-MANDIBU, JEDI SEER

The path of the Jedi is one of harmony, one that avoids violence and seeks to unite living beings through the peace of the Force. Jedi Guardians are needed to prevent the spread of evil, but it is the Jedi Consulars who uphold the central precepts of the Jedi Code.

The most esteemed Jedi Consular Masters serve on the Reconciliation Council, which is responsible for negotiating with political factions both within the Republic and outside it. We are not a replacement for the Senate. In fact, we serve at its pleasure. Yet our understanding of the Force gives us a unique perspective in conflict resolution, one that ensures the galaxy's long-term stability.

Hundreds of years with the Order, and remain a diplomat I do. —Yoda

While the High Council reports to the Supreme Chancellor, the Reconciliation Council often works with the Republic Diplomatic Corps. The Jedi are largely synonymous with the Republic, and it is not uncommon for new alien cultures to insist on dealing with a Jedi representative when negotiating their world's entry into the galactic community. Jedi Consulars help to serve all people of the galaxy in political dealings

4.11 A JEDI CONSULAR USES WORDS AND WITS TO RESOLVE CONFLICTS.

and conflict resolutions. While the Force is a significant part of our effectiveness and is useful in detecting deception, using the Force to prod warring parties to sign a treaty is considered an abuse of a Jedi's power.

Besides negotiating, Jedi Consulars also research and teach. Many can be found on Coruscant taking advantage of the Archives' voluminous data records, while others serve on such hubs of information as Obroa-skai and Telos.

Profound skill with the Force is the mark of a Jedi Consular. The most advanced among us are given the honorific of Sage Master. The greatest healers, seers, and prophets have all come from within our ranks. Consulars can be outstanding fighters if pushed, but are more likely to rely on Force talents such as affect mind or telekinesis than on brandishing a lightsaber. Though a Jedi Consular does carry a lightsaber, typically bearing a green blade, it usually remains hooked on his or her belt.

If you have chosen the path of the Jedi Consular, your empathic talents are strong and you have a deep connection to the Force.

4.12 MEDIATING AN END TO WARS CAN SAVE THE LIVES OF BILLIONS.

Throughout your career you will improve thousands of lives through your actions.

JEDI SEER

Among the ranks of the Jedi Consulars is that of a Jedi Seer. This is the calling I have followed in my own life, so it is one I understand well. Those who become seers are attuned to the higher workings of the Unifying Force and can perceive how it binds space and time into a coherent and breathtaking meshwork. Seers hear the voice and feel the will of the Force. They can view events from remote distances, and receive visions from both the past and the future. Some seers, known as Jedi Prophets, are gifted with extraordinary foreknowledge.

YODA TAUGHT ME THERE ARE LIMITS TO PROPHECY— BUT HE ALSO URGED ME NOT TO IGNORE IT. —LUKE

Their divinations are recorded in our Holocrons.

The connection between the Jedi Seers and the Unifying Force is the most important asset the Jedi Order possesses. Other powerful groups, including the Hutts, employ warriors, martial artists, and pilots—but who besides the Jedi can perceive the entirety of existence?

How many foresaw their downfall? Not a one. Fools.

4.14 Jedi Healers treat the wounded on battlefields after the fighting has ceased.

Jedi Healer

As the seers use their connection to the Unifying Force, Jedi Healers use their connection to the Living Force to save the lives of the dying and to cure the infected. They work closely with the Jedi Medical Corps but are full-fledged Jedi Knights and Masters (as opposed to most MedCorps Jedi, who never achieved the rank of Padawan). In this leadership role, they oversee the Temple's infirmary and practice their curative trade on worlds such as Rhinnal and H'ratth.

WITH THE SEPARATISTS DIGGING IN ON THE RIM, WE NEED ONE HEALER PER BATTLE FORMATION AT MINIMUM.
-AHSOKA

4.13 The Jedi Seers are responsible for the prophecy of the Chosen One.

4.15 Jedi Astronomers study stars, nebulae, quasars, and black holes.

Jedi Researcher

Jedi Researchers employ their exceptional minds to solve theoretical problems and improve the quality of data in our Archives. Specialists among their ranks include mathematicians, hyperspatial physicists, astronomers, and biologists like the esteemed Master Bowspritz.

Jedi Ambassador

The Jedi Consular does battle using words and ideas. Nowhere is this more apparent than in the specialization of ambassador. Ever since the Jedi learned and adapted the principles of justice from ancient Caamasi philosophers, we have been known for our impartiality. The precepts of the Jedi Code insist on fair-mindedness: *There is no passion, there is serenity. There is no chaos, there is harmony.*

This attitude is what makes Jedi Consulars the preferred representatives of the Galactic Republic, and many of us hold the title of Jedi Ambassador within the Republic bureaucracy. Jedi Ambassadors work closely with government officials, and are the face of the Republic to those they meet. They are held to the highest standards of civilized behavior.

Sometimes Master Dooku just stares down the negotiators. It usually works. Q-G

4.16 Hespecia Tik'kla, the Caamasi lawgiver who inspired the Jedi approach to justice

Jedi Diplomat

Jedi Diplomats are a related class, and are more numerous than ambassadors. They work in a more active and less symbolic role, hammering out the terms of agreements and upholding the new galactic peace. It is important to remember that in diplomacy, flexibility is strength. A rigid tree will be uprooted in the first windstorm. By enacting a treaty, a diplomat can end hostilities and save billions of lives—a far greater victory than any warrior could earn on a battlefield.

LEIA COULD BE AMONG THE BEST IN THIS AREA, IF I COULD JUST GET HER TO TRAIN ONCE IN A WHILE.
-LUKE

Lore Keeper

Lore Keeper is a broad term that encompasses Jedi historians, Jedi librarians, and Jedi archivists. Historians specialize in the study of prior eras, while librarians interact with visiting scholars and make the Archives' resources accessible to all Jedi. Archivists translate, copy, and store all new texts added to the Temple's collection. All three types of Lore Keepers are part of the Librarians Assembly, a Temple organization governing the acquisition of data.

Do the Archives really contain everything? Somehow it seems rude to question this point.
-Kenobi

4.17 Lore Keepers transcribe ancient texts and debate the finer points of translation.

JEDI SENTINEL

I suspect the majority of the Jedi survivors still at large belong to the Sentinel class.

BY MORRIT CH'GALLY, JEDI RECRUITER

Striking a balance between the Guardian and the Consular, the Jedi Sentinel is a class that combines both disciplines with civilian expertise. Because we don't focus our time on lightsaber exercises or Force meditation, we Sentinels have acquired a host of skills that don't require Force sensitivity—and we can accomplish tasks that neither the Guardians nor the Consulars could handle on their own.

One of the unspoken truths of the Jedi is that we are insulated from the workings of the galaxy. In my view, it's possible to know *too* much about combat or the Force—if it means that you know next to nothing about intelligence gathering, computer slicing, technological surveillance, or espionage. Sentinels approach these disciplines from the bottom up without assuming that the Force will reveal all the answers. When you do this, you'll find there's a great deal the civilians of the galaxy can teach us.

4.18 A JEDI SENTINEL HAS THE SKILLS TO HANDLE THE UNEXPECTED.

Unlike Consulars and Guardians who travel between trouble spots, Jedi Sentinels often remain tied to a single sector or planetary system for months or years at a time. In previous eras, this led many Sentinels to be appointed Jedi Watchmen where they took on responsibility for the welfare of a defined region of space.

Though Sentinels rarely need to use a weapon, like all Jedi they carry a lightsaber. A Sentinel's lightsaber usually bears a yellow blade. Haven't seen many of those? Now you know how few we are in

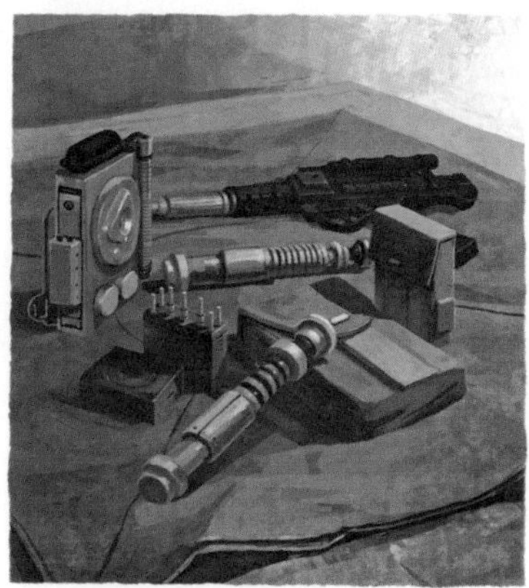

4.19 Sentinels often carry blasters as well as power cells and other specialist's tools.

number, and how well we stay concealed until action is required.

Because the Jedi Sentinels fill the gap between Guardians and Consulars, we tackle missions for which neither group is optimized. But in truth, Sentinels often get the jobs that neither group *wants*. Handling assignments that our colleagues have written off as impossible is the sign of a Sentinel.

MOST OF MY STUDENTS HAD OTHER LIVES PRIOR TO JOINING MY ORDER. BECAUSE THEY COME FROM DIVERSE BACKGROUNDS, THEY POSSESS MANY OF THESE SKILLS.
-LUKE

The ranks of Jedi Sentinels include investigators, spies, tech specialists, saboteurs, and other experts whose talents don't easily fit into the Order's traditions. Jedi recruiters, such as myself, typically start out as investigators before using those same talents to identify and enroll Force-sensitive children from across the Republic. Our jobs require broad skill sets, but Jedi Sentinels don't care where a tactic originated as long as it works.

Slicer

Slicers are computer specialists who are able to infiltrate networks while leaving no trace of their manipulation. As with many Sentinel specializations, this skill is notable due to the fact that the Force doesn't really offer a shortcut. While you might use a mind trick to get past the guard, once you're seated at a terminal your data skill is the only thing that matters.

Tech Expert

The tech expert has carved out a unique talent among the ranks of Jedi, who often shun leading-edge technology. They have broader skill sets than slicers, and are able to disassemble, juice up, and rebuild any piece of equipment from a hyperdrive engine to an electronic deck of sabacc cards. Due to the prevalence of maintenance and repair droids, these abilities are rare among the Jedi Order. Some tech experts have cultivated a gift for the Force ability *mechu-deru*, which bestows on

NO KIDDING! I HAVE TO TAKE APART AND REASSEMBLE THE TEMPLE DROIDS JUST TO KEEP MY SKILLS UP TO DATE.
Anakin

ISN'T THIS WHY WE KEEP ARTOO AROUND?
-AHSOKA

4.20 A Jedi gifted in *mechu-deru* can sense the complex structure of technology.

the user an intuitive understanding of how complicated structures, including machinery and circuitry, fit together.

Security Expert

The security expert is known for his or her ability to disarm traps and silence alarms. This Jedi recognizes the Force's limitations when it comes to technological countermeasures, and has saved many missions and lives by studying how to disrupt them. A security expert can be the difference between a successful infiltration and a lifelong prison sentence in the flame-dungeons of Nal Hutta.

THEY CAN BE ON MY TEAM SO I NEVER END UP HERE! -AHSOKA

Jedi Shadows

The elite Jedi Shadows are widely respected members of the Sentinels. The role of Jedi Shadows is to seek out and vanquish any traces of the dark side, requiring them to be both spies and saboteurs. Jedi Shadows prize the mission above all else, and often must make moral compromises that would be unpleasant for other members of the Order.

KATARN WOULD HAVE BEEN AN OUTSTANDING SENTINEL. KAM, TOO. -LUKE

4.21 Jedi Shadows serve to uphold the ways of the Force by hunting down agents of the dark side.

Alter Abilities

By Sabla-Mandibu, Jedi Seer

As a youngling you learned Control; as a Padawan you studied Sense; and now as a Knight your education in the Force will continue in the discipline of Alter. These abilities, which use the Force to physically impact the surrounding environment, are the most difficult to master. But without Alter, you are like a mud limpet—perceiving your world but incapable of touching it. With Alter, you will grow arms and legs. Learn these skills, practice them daily, and you will deepen your aptitude for Alter throughout your career.

Who are you calling a mud limpet? —Thame

4.22 Small replicas of the Muntuur Stones are used by beginners.

Telekinesis is the most fundamental Alter ability, forming the basis for the familiar Force push and Force pull. Your training should focus on both precision and control, but also on lifting great weights. The oxygen bottle is a fine exercise for precision, since it requires a Jedi to fill an empty bottle with oxygen molecules plucked one by one from the air. For control, visit the Temple's Kuddaka chamber, where the Muntuur Stones are kept. Each stone weighs several tons, so merely jostling one can be marked as a success. Master Fae, it should be noted, can levitate all six after entering a state of deep meditation.

Impressive! While size matters not, only five can I lift since I passed 700. —Yoda

Affect mind, commonly referred to as the "Jedi mind trick," can override the impulses of an undisciplined brain. This ability should be a temporary means to accomplish a greater good. It should never be used for profit or gain.

I think master Qui-Gon is a little too fond of this.
-Kenobi

Alter abilities can be used to heal others, but also to injure. Both are Jedi abilities, though the latter must be used sparingly because the potential for abuse is so great. Among the Sith, **Force injure** was used without reservation to kill others from a distance.

Alter Environment describes a family of abilities that stand as evidence of the Force's ability to control the natural world. With this a Jedi can summon a whirlwind or a lightning strike, or can direct hailstorms and crashing waves against the walls of an enemy fortification.

I'VE HEARD THAT SOME MASTERS CAN CALL DOWN A PILLAR OF FIRE!
Anakin

The related ability of **plant surge**, or *Consitor Sato*, is among my favorites. By drawing on the Living Force, a Jedi can ensnare enemies in a nest of thorny vines and end a conflict with minimal violence.

THIS COULD HAVE COME IN HANDY ON AQUARIS!
-AHSOKA

4.23 By using Alter Environment, a Jedi can turn a nearby body of water into a weapon.

Advanced Force Techniques

While some Jedi have demonstrated their mastery of the Force's more challenging expressions, this does not obligate you to follow their lead. But, if your talents lie in similar areas, you may wish to devote a year or two of your knighthood to becoming an expert in an advanced Force technique.

I'VE HEARD ABOUT A RECRUITMENT DRIVE FOR BATTLE MEDITATION ADEPTS. SEEMS THE COUNCIL IS WORRIED AFTER WHAT HAPPENED ON NABOO.

Anakin

Battle meditation, in study and practice, is actively encouraged by the Council and is absolutely critical to wartime victories. Through battle meditation a Jedi touches the minds of every soldier in a combat zone, friend and foe alike. Allies gain a boost in morale and fighting efficiency, while enemies become seized by confusion and fear. At the Battle of Mizra, the death of the Jedi coordinator to a Sith sniper turned the Jedi retreat into a full-scale slaughter.

Combustion, or *Flamusfracta*, is a severe culmination of the art of telekinesis by which a Jedi causes objects to explode. The intensity of the blast can injure an entire room of enemies, particularly if the affected object is made of flammable material.

Mere child's play.

Art of the Small is a fascinating method of melding oneself with the Force. Under meditation, a Jedi's Force presence is shrunk to that of a single atom, allowing for an unprecedented degree of stealth as well as allowing for a perception of the universe on a molecular scale. Using telekinesis in this state allows Jedi to eliminate toxins and cure certain ailments in others as well as in themselves by constructing healthy proteins and rebuilding cells.

Doppelganger, or *Similfuturus*, permits a Jedi to create a short-lived duplicate of himself or herself or an external object that is visually indistinguishable from the real item. Those who have perfected this ability can create phantoms of any person of their choosing or trick an enemy into seeing more objects, such as droids, than are actually present.

4.24 Doppelganger is an effective technique for confusing or misleading an opponent.

WONDER IF THIS WOULD WORK ON A WHOLE ARMY OF CLONES?

-AHSOKA

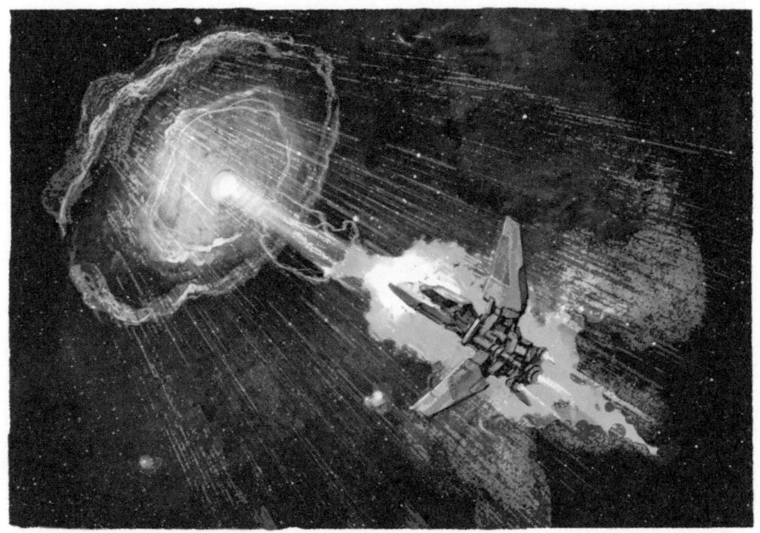

4.25 THE CREATION OF A HYPERSPACE WORMHOLE IS A POWERFUL USE OF THE FORCE THAT CAN SEND SHOCKWAVES THROUGH SPACE.

The **Force Storm** is truly an awe-inspiring demonstration of pure natural energy. After using the Force to open a hyperspace wormhole, tremendous shocks will ripple through the fabric of space. Due to the Force Storm's potential for abuse, the Council has recently classified it as a dark side power.

THE REBORN EMPEROR USED THIS AT DA SOOCHA. IT HAS THE POWER TO KILL WORLDS.
-LUKE

Yes—the Jedi limit, the Sith embrace. And now we have unlimited power.

Forbidden Force Techniques

In your heart, you know which abilities run counter to the Jedi Code. Yet during the last war, the raw power wielded by the Sith prompted some Jedi to match them in rage. Such miscalculations always end in tragedy.

Forbidden Force techniques are marked by a loss of control. Using any of these techniques as a Jedi Knight is prohibited.

Force Grip This refinement of telekinesis works as an invisible extension of the hand, allowing Force-users to hoist enemies into the air or close off the air from their tracheas. It is truly a brutal and cruel application of the Force.

IS IT REALLY THAT DANGEROUS? HOW CAN IT BE A DARK SIDE MOVE IF YOU JUST LIFT SOMEBODY.
Anakin

BY THEIR NECK? AND HE LECTURES ME ABOUT MY ANGER.
-AHSOKA

Force Insanity This dark side perversion of affect mind invades a victim's psyche with sinister energies to the point that he or she becomes paralyzed by horror. The technique can push vulnerable intellects into permanent madness.

Deadly Sight A tactic that was once extremely rare, even among the Sith, exploded in usage during the last decades of the war. By channeling this ability, a Force-user can harness fury and hatred and then project them through an intense glare onto a victim—as long as that victim is in the practitioner's range of vision. Deadly Sight has been known to blister skin and vaporize extremities.

Morichro Though it is practiced by some Jedi Masters, it is considered off-limits for Knights. By using Morichro, a Jedi can slow the body functions of another being into mild catatonia or long-term suspended animation. There is great risk that an untrained user may go too far and accidentally stop a heart from beating.

Emerald Lightning A technique in which a Jedi can spray electric bolts of variable intensity from the hands and fingers. This technique is closely related to the dark side power of Sith Lightning, but it springs from a sense of determined justice and has been studied by some Masters under controlled conditions. Its energies can also be contained in a ball of pure kinetic force known as a kinetite.

VADER EXHIBITED THIS POWER, ON MIMBAN.
-LUKE

Advanced Lightsaber Techniques

By Skarch Vaunk, Jedi Battlemaster

Form VII Lightsaber Combat: *Juyo*

Juyo has existed for thousands of years but is the most controversial of all forms, and most of you will have no need to learn it. *Juyo* is nicknamed the Way of the Vornskr, but in my view it is best described by its alternate title, the Ferocity Form.

Vicious and unpredictable, Form VII requires a Jedi to attack under the guidance of controlled passion. It is this aspect that has caused the most consternation among the Order, for proper execution of *Juyo* seemingly puts a Jedi in violation of one of the Code's core precepts: *There is no emotion, there is peace.*

Not a surprise, Jedi. It is a Sith style.

However, Form VII masters do not give themselves to emotion blindly. They channel their inner turmoil into a mental forge, which provides the passion to power their raw and furious strikes. A true expert keeps the emotions locked within the forge. Lesser practitioners of the art might allow their emotions to spill out during battle, poisoning their intentions and drawing them into the fury of a dark side rage.

4.26 A key component to Form VII is the ability to use inner emotion to give strength to the moves.

For this reason *Juyo* is restricted by the Council. I accept only a handful of students—handpicked according to my personal standards—each year. Never again will I permit the widespread use of this form after the events of the last Sith War, when *Juyo* provided the trigger for Jedi to sink into butchery and join the ranks of the Sith.

Form VII is difficult to master. Its movements are sharp and chaotic, and occur in quick bursts. You can drill these sequences into your head through regular practice, but you will not truly be using *Juyo* until you allow excitement, passion, and rage to color your actions.

While its attacks can eviscerate defenses—even the blocks of a Form III master—Form VII leaves its practitioner vulnerable and open to counterattack. Multiple opponents can overwhelm a *Juyo* master by exploiting a moment's vulnerability. Force shoves and pulls are also effective at rattling a Form VII defense.

Master Windu has developed a variant of Form VII called Vaapad. Qui-Gon won't let me study it. -Kenobi

NOBODY'S ALLOWED TO STUDY VAAPAD. -AHSOKA

4.27 Basic Form VII drills

ADDITIONAL LIGHTSABER TECHNIQUES

As a Knight you should never stop learning—lightsaber techniques are no different. Every move you perfect only opens pathways to new moves. Even we battlemasters are humbled by how little we truly understand. Here are a few of the more advanced moves you should study in your knighthood.

Saber Throw is a difficult discipline to perfect. Combining the physicality of lightsaber combat with the telekinesis of Force Alter, it allows you to hurl a lit saber at a target and call it back to your hand. A saber may be thrown in a pinwheeling motion, or in a straight line as a spear. Use the Force to help guide the saber's path and extend its range beyond what your strength would normally permit. Many of the Order's best practitioners are stationed on the parapets of the Temple as Jedi Snipers.

THIS MOVE STRIKES ME AS DESPERATE AND RISKY. MY SABER SHOULDN'T NEED TO LEAVE MY HAND.
—DOOKU

Mounted combat is the art of fighting from a saddle. This may involve a speeder bike or an animal such as a hornagaunt. Either way it requires an understanding of how to steer and manage your speed while fighting. You must also learn how to take advantage of your higher elevation relative to ground-level targets. Remember that if you are riding a living creature, it may become necessary to calm the beast through the Force lest it become panicked by the sounds and smells of battle.

On my thirty-third kybuck I am.
—Yoda

4.28 A MOUNTED JEDI ALWAYS HAS THE HIGH GROUND.

In **trakata**, a Jedi can take advantage of one of the lightsaber's unique abilities—the ability to be rapidly switched off and on. In "Passing the Blade," a Jedi shuts down the saber to momentarily bypass an enemy's block, then immediately reactivates it for a killing strike. If two combatants have locked their sabers together, a trained Jedi may choose to deactivate his or her saber and throw the enemy off balance.

Sokan encourages a Jedi to use the surrounding terrain as a weapon, from seeking the high ground to taking cover behind obstacles. An enemy can be driven back into hazards such as active machinery or open pits. I do not consider Sokan a distinct lightsaber form, but some find merit in this style. Sokan is best employed on a Jedi's "home territory," where the ground is familiar and holds no surprises.

4.29 Through the use of trakata, you can bypass your opponent's defenses and land a Mark of Contact.

EVEN MORE TECHNIQUES: THE MAJESTRIX OF SKYE DEVELOPED TRISPZEST, WHICH IS A FORM OF AERIAL SWORDPLAY USED BY HER WINGED WARRIORS. —LUKE

Developing Your Own Style

As a Jedi who has reached the rank of Knight, you have received instruction in Forms I–VI combat. By now you have undoubtedly settled on one that suits your physical strengths as well as your battle philosophy. Some Jedi are content to stay within this framework, and this is admirable. The traditional Forms have existed for millennia, and each has many thousands of advocates.

Yet some Jedi may find advantage in a hybrid style that draws upon any or all forms. Guardians who spend most of their time honing their bodies may choose to combine the strength of Form V with the acrobatics of Form IV, while Consulars accustomed to the "diplomat's style" of Form VI may find it illuminating to study its pure root, Form III. It is always advised to have one "home stance" with attacks and parries you know well, a stance you can return to whenever you become disoriented or need to regroup against a grueling enemy.

I now see the vulnerabilities of Form IV, and think it could be made safer with a touch of Form III.

-Kenobi

DABBLER IN ALL, MASTER OF NONE. MY FOCUS REMAINS ON MAKASHI.

—DOOKU

4.30 By combining unique elements from the different forms, Jedi may develop their own style.

Lightsaber combat can be both physical and mental, as you test an enemy's defenses and adjust your approach. But a duel can also be psychological. *Dun Möch* is the act of using words to break an opponent's concentration and shatter his or her morale. By urging enemies to surrender, or telling them they have no hope of success, a Jedi can end a fight without bloodshed. But be warned—too much taunting can lead a Jedi down the dark path.

YES—AN ADDED WEAPON I SHALL PERFECT. —DOOKU

Every Jedi must find his or her own balance and method of fighting. If your style is unique and has sufficient complexity it may one day be recognized as a new subset and be taught to future classes of Initiates and Padawans. Perhaps even with your name attached to it.

I'd like to make my own style! Think I'll get a training droid that's programmed for all of these.
-Thame

ENLISTING NEW MEMBERS

BY MORRIT CH'GALLY, JEDI RECRUITER

The Jedi, as you well know, forbid romantic attachment. We do not marry, nor do we breed powerful lineages from our greatest members. How then do we survive from generation to generation, or rebuild our numbers after the decimation of war?

The Force supplies the answer. Any being, regardless of homeworld, species, wealth, or the social status of his or her family, can be born with the ability to touch the Force. These beings have a gift, and if we don't teach them how to use it, the Jedi Order is responsible for squandering that gift.

In fact, those who don't learn how to harness their talents at a young age may come to view the Force as a curse. On some planets, those who are Force sensitive may be persecuted as demonic magicians, or may become so enamored with their otherworldly powers that they become exactly the monsters their neighbors fear. Once they have reached such a state it is difficult to bring them into the light of Jedi teachings, which in past decades has made them easy marks for the Sith.

Master Unskette and I tried to recruit a child on Orto, but the parents threw stones at us. Referred the case to the council. -Thame

THE COUNCIL KEEPS DATA ON FORCE-STRONG CHILDREN IN THE KYBER CRYSTAL. I DOUBT IT'S COMPLETE, THOUGH. -AHSOKA

4.31 It is best to recognize and recruit Force-sensitives while they are still infants.

NOBODY NOTICED ME UNTIL I WAS NINE. MANY FORCE-SENSITIVES MUST SLIP THROUGH THE CRACKS. Anakin

Correct! There is much potential for the dark side in those who are forgotten.

The responsible use of power takes a lifetime to perfect, and therefore the Jedi Order only rarely accepts members who are older than a few years. Most of you came to the Temple as infants.

Locating Force-strong newborns is a straightforward process, at least within the Republic's borders. Mandatory blood tests performed at birth record the concentration of midi-chlorians in an infant's cells, and positive results are forwarded to the Jedi Temple for follow-up. Because midi-chlorian analysis is not always definitive—particularly among older children or beings with unusual physiologies—special tools or puzzles may be employed instead. These include the testing screen, a tool that records a subject's ability to read minds or view images remotely, and the mental maze, a test that demonstrates whether a subject can use rudimentary telekinesis.

Portable blood scanners are now available in the quartermaster's office. I carry several. Q-G

MISPERCEPTIONS OF THE JEDI

The job of a Jedi Recruiter can be thankless. While many families are proud to have their offspring chosen by the Force, the practical reality of taking a child away from his or her parents is messy and unpleasant. We Jedi firmly believe that Force-strong beings have a right to receive the best training available, and our

4.32 A GIFTED CHILD CAN DETECT A FORCE-IMBUED OBJECT FROM OTHER, SIMILAR OBJECTS.

I WILL NOT DO THIS. MEMBERSHIP AND RECRUITMENT IN MY ORDER IS STRICTLY VOLUNTARY.
—LUKE

way requires shunning emotional commitment, especially toward one's birth family. Yet something that seems self-evident to us has been characterized as monstrous in the HoloNet. I admit that while we recruiters are vital to the continuation of the Order, we don't do much to burnish the Order's reputation.

The following are perennial slurs leveled against the Order. As a Jedi Knight you must do your part to counter these lies, not by arguing but by setting an example of selflessness and service.

The Jedi are sorcerers. Popular on primitive worlds and among adherents of certain religious sects, this belief betrays a misunderstanding of the Force's presence throughout the universe. The Force is a real, demonstrable phenomenon, not a twist of forbidden "magic." Through our connection to the Force, the Jedi are the agents of life itself.

The Jedi are kidnappers. An all too familiar accusation for Jedi Recruiters, this charge springs from the pain of emotional attachment. It is also technically false. Within the Republic, the Jedi Order has the legal authority to take custody of Force-sensitives, and some Masters have argued that the Force's presence in a child indicates the child's consent to join the Order even before he or she is able to speak.

The Jedi are brainwashers. This belief is in part due to the secrecy surrounding Jedi training and in part due to a widespread misunderstanding of the so-called Jedi mind trick. Some claim that the Order is responsible for mass hypnosis and mind-control. Patently untrue.

The Jedi are elitists. It is fashionable to equate the presence of midi-chlorians with genetic superiority, but the Force *chose* to manifest itself through the symbiosis in our cells. The Force can call anyone, and is thus the very definition of egalitarian.

Hatred of the Jedi ran deep, and few mourned them when they were gone.

THE HISTORY OF THE SITH

BY RESTELLY QUIST, CHIEF LIBRARIAN

The dark side is the selfish, impulsive energy you feel when you have not set yourself at peace. Members of the Order who give themselves over to these destructive emotions often experience an irreversible spiritual corruption that marks them as a dark sider. Those who follow the rituals of a *specific* dark side philosophy become Sith. Not all dark siders are Sith, though the Sith have proven to be the most persuasive and malevolent power of the past several millennia. At times they have controlled the majority of the galaxy.

Chilling. The Sith were the enemies of life.
Q-G

4-33 THE SITH ARE EXTINCT BUT ECHOES OF THEIR EVIL REMAIN.

The Sith hold fast to a set of beliefs influenced by the necrotic magic of the alien species whose name they share, but their core tenets are summarized in the Sith Code:

Peace is a lie, there is only passion
Through passion I gain strength
Through strength I gain power
Through power I gain victory
Through victory my chains are broken
The Force shall free me

The Sith hold that these beliefs represent their willingness to challenge the restrictions of orthodoxy and shake the foundations of power. Yet it is plain that the Sith Code is a selfish one. Every tenet focuses on individual wants and desires. The Jedi know that greatness can only be won through humbling oneself. The Sith settle for quick-and-easy power by sinking deep into their emotions.

The Sith species, originating on Korriban, and the earliest dark siders, those who broke away from the Order during the First Great Schism on Tython, shared similar outlooks on power. Eventually their teachings became so intertwined that "Sith" came to describe any adherent to their beliefs, regardless of species.

The Sith carry red-bladed lightsabers, caused by their use of synthetic crystals. These lightsabers serve to both announce their presence and to test our own sabers in battle. The blade of a Sith saber has been known to "break" the blade of a Jedi saber by overloading its energy matrix. The annihilation of the Sith Order has thankfully put an end to such duels.

A feature rarely needed. A true Sith can kill a Jedi in moments.

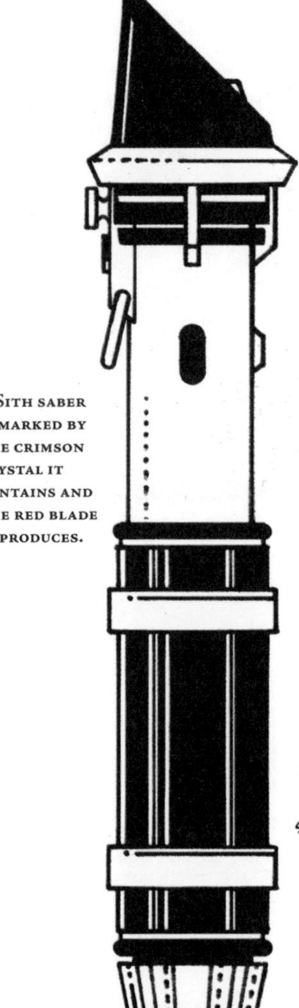

4.34 A Sith saber is marked by the crimson crystal it contains and the red blade it produces.

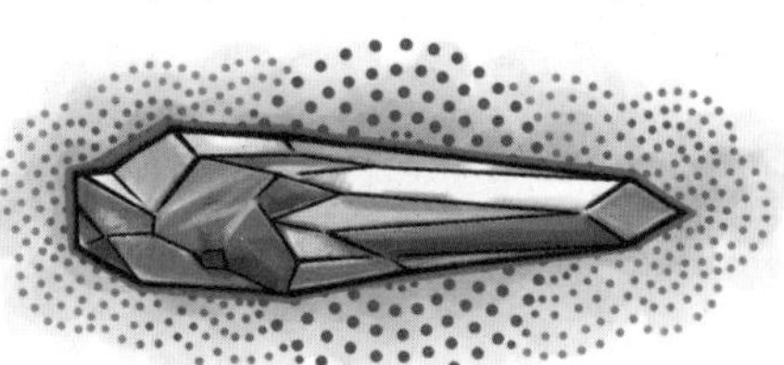

4.35 The Sith forge crimson crystals through synthetic means.

Gone the Sith are, though dark siders remain. One on Dennogra was I forced to kill.

—Yoda

THE SECOND GREAT SCHISM AND THE FINAL WAR

Still live on Syngia some monstrosities do. Properly warned, all Knights should be. —Yoda

Modern Sith came about after the Second Great Schism and the Hundred-Year Darkness—a war between Jedi and dark siders that involved the alchemical creation of monsters. The victorious Jedi sentenced the surviving dark siders to banishment. But among the uncharted stars the exiled Jedi discovered the Sith species, who worshipped death and the angry energies of the dark side. They became the Lords of the Sith, merging their fallen Jedi culture with the sacrificial rituals of the savage Korriban natives.

4.36 DARK JEDI USED ALCHEMY TO CREATE MONSTERS DURING THE SECOND GREAT SCHISM.

Two thousand years later, the Lords of Sith Space mounted an invasion of the Republic. Running wild over Kirrek and Coruscant, the Sith blitzed the heart of civilized space before the Jedi could drive them back into exile. This was the first of many wars between the Jedi and Sith.

During the Vultar Cataclysm in the Third Great Schism, dark siders influenced by the Sith triggered the obliteration of an entire world. This act led to regular clashes between the dark and the light, including the Great Sith War of Exar Kun and the Jedi Civil War that saw the defection of two Jedi champions—who became Darth Malak and Darth Revan. The Jedi Order barely survived these conflicts. So only a few centuries later, when war broke

EXAR KUN LIVED ON AS A DARK SIDE SPIRIT. HE NEARLY KILLED ME, BUT IT TAUGHT ME NOT TO UNDERESTIMATE THE SITH. —LUKE

INTERESTING— I HAVE READ THAT REVAN RETURNED TO THE LIGHT BEFORE HIS SUDDEN DISAPPEARANCE FROM GALACTIC AFFAIRS. —DOOKU

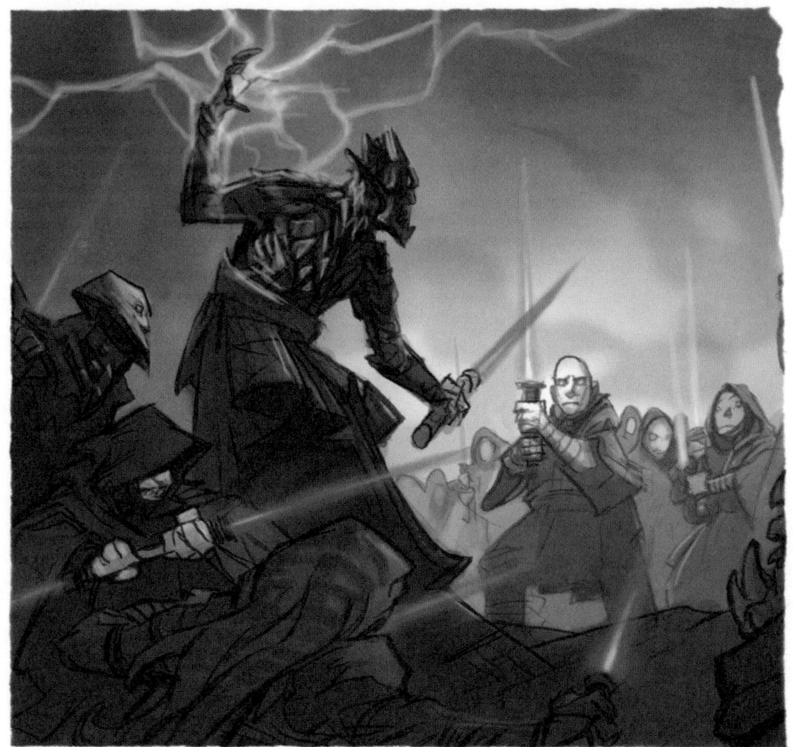

4.37 THE SITH'S DEFEAT AT THE BATTLE OF RUUSAN MARKED THE END OF THE DARK AGE.

out again, the Sith took control of Coruscant, relocating the Jedi to Tython. We have since won back our rightful place on Coruscant.

The Fourth Great Schism, which occurred a millennium ago, brought on a thousand years of fighting, the ascendance of Darth Ruin and the Sith, and the plague that provided the drumbeat for what was truly the Republic's Dark Age. It was a military campaign that nearly brought an end to civilization. Yet the Army of Light beat the Brotherhood of Darkness at the Battle of Ruusan. Those Jedi who sacrificed their lives have transformed the Dark Age into a new Golden Age of peace and bounty.

TOO BAD IT COULDN'T LAST.
-AHSOKA

Darkness do
I sometimes sense.
Vigilant the Jedi must remain.
—Yoda

Darth Bane and the End of the Sith

The Sith have been the enemies of the Jedi for thousands of years, yet outsiders who viewed them as an inevitable—and even a necessary—counterbalance to the light side were proven wrong after the Battle of Ruusan when the Sith Order crumbled. Although danger still lurks among the stars, the citizens of the Republic need no longer fear the title of *Darth*.

Idle rumors say the Sith survived under the "Rule of Two"—one master, one apprentice. —Dooku

It is ironic that one of their own, Darth Bane, helped bring about the destruction of the Sith—but it is not surprising. It is the Sith way to scratch and claw for power. In the war's last decade, Bane rose through the ranks of the Brotherhood of Darkness to challenge the leadership of Sith Lord Kaan. From the Sith prisoners in custody on Akrit'tar, we have learned that many of them considered Bane to be the *Sith'ari*—the culmination of a prophecy that foretold the rise of a perfect being. This divination, an inverted mirror of the Jedi prophecy of the Chosen One, reflected the Sith need to cast their hopes upon a savior as the Jedi Army of Light closed in on them. Bane's popularity split the ranks of the Sith Lords, causing them to lose focus and to surrender key ground at Ruusan. Ultimately, Lord Kaan knew he could not win and triggered a Thought Bomb. This unspeakable dark side weapon scorched the surface of Ruusan and drew the spirits of every combatant, Jedi *and* Sith, into its bottomless singularity.

One dead, on Naboo! —Anakin

Can't we shut down the Separatists first? —Ahsoka

Bane died with the rest of the Sith Lords on Ruusan, proving that not even the *Sith'ari* could sustain an order founded on aggression and greed. Though we Jedi must continue to resist the temptations of the dark side, it is cause for good cheer that the enemies of life have at last been vanquished.

4.38 Darth Bane

Jedi ignorance is breathtaking. The viper lay in plain view, and none suspected.

Other Dark Side Organizations

Fallen Jedi and those who hold the views of the Sith are only two types of followers of the dark side. There are other paths that can corrupt those who are Force sensitive. Just as there are rival organizations to the Jedi, there exist cults and sects whose sole purpose is the exploitation of the dark side for selfish means.

I don't see potential for recruitment here. The Navy can contain Tund.

The **Sorcerers of Tund** are believed to be descendants of pure-blooded Sith exiled from Korriban long ago. Deep in the Outer Rim's Centrality, they practice a secretive and malevolent style of Force manipulation, which they characterize as spellcasting. The Council has tried to recruit them, but without success.

The Force-using tradition of the **Jarvashqiine** extends to the earliest centuries of the Republic. Their shamans believed that the dark side can manifest itself only through elaborate blood rituals. But removing these atavistic rites can actually block a Jarvashqiine adept's ability to use the Force.

The **Mecrosa Order** originated among House Mecetti in the Tapani sector. Its dark side practitioners have persisted in the subsequent centuries as outspoken challengers to Jedi teachings.

The **Bladeborn** are a splinter faction of Sith who believe in the superiority of edged weapons as a means of focusing the dark side. Their tools include traditional lightsabers as well as exotic vibroblades such as the Sith Tremor sword.

Early in the last war, the Dark Underlord raised an army of **Black Knights**. Though they fell in battle to the Jedi, the Black Knights have risen again and again over the centuries and may not be entirely silent even today.

Rose again they did, during the Flumhaka revolt. An adventure for me, as a new Padawan it was.
—Yoda

THREATS TO JEDI TEACHINGS

BY RESTELLY QUIST, CHIEF LIBRARIAN

The postwar Republic reformation has reshaped the Jedi Order. We have learned much from the previous thousand years—from the fall of Phanius and the war he ignited to our final victory at Ruusan. The loss of so many Jedi to Sith seductions has prompted the enactment of new rules governing Jedi teachings. The Council no longer exhibits tolerance toward heretics who believe they have found a superior path that runs counter to the Jedi Order's 24,000 years of accumulated wisdom.

Yet the Sith are older and run deeper.

4.39 FOLLOW THE TEACHINGS OF THE COUNCIL AND YOU WILL NOT JOIN THE LOST.

The Sith and fallen Jedi are not under discussion here, for their evil is apparent to all. But alternate philosophies can be just as tragically misguided. At the forefront of these philosophies are the **relativists**, those who argue that the dark side does not exist. Many Padawans seem to go through a similar phase, and as their Masters, you must set them straight or they may carry their misperceptions into adulthood. These radicals do not deny the existence of dark side powers, but maintain that the darkness only manifests in the mind of the individual Force-wielder. The dangers in this philosophy are clear. Those who believe that *any* action can be taken—so long as one's intent is pure—soon believe their intent is always right.

Corrected these Padawans must be or clouded their futures will be. —Yoda

The so-called **gray Jedi** have been with us since the beginning. Although they do not break with the Jedi orthodoxy concerning the dark side, they bristle when asked to take orders from the Council. Gray Jedi make compromises, cut corners, and hide their actions from scrutiny, all under the assumption that their experience makes them authorities on policy. They are mavericks who are difficult to control, but can be valued members of the Order after they have been persuaded to follow the established hierarchy.

The Lost is a term applied to Jedi Masters who have resigned from the Order for philosophical reasons. Although few in number, the Lost represent a failing of the Jedi to keep our greatest thinkers within our fold. Their loss is our shame.

Their loss is my asset!

THEY CALL IT THE LOST TWENTY NOW—DOOKU WAS THE LATEST. WISH I KNEW WHAT HAPPENED. Anakin

NOT ME. LET'S JUST STOP THIS CREEP! -AHSOKA

Some call Master Qui-Gon a gray Jedi, and I confess I can see why they do. He's going to get me into trouble. -Kenobi

INTERESTING—WONDER IF HE DID. -LUKE

I have encountered many such groups, including the Cruthauses and the Boughtine. The Force finds a way to express itself. Q-G

OTHER FORCE-USING ORGANIZATIONS

The Jedi Order is not the only organization to study and follow the Force. Countless schools have arisen among cultures that have the perception to hear the Force's call—from the Followers of Palawa to the Order of Dai Bendu and the Chatos Academy. While these are admirable efforts, it is our conviction that the Jedi Order is the ideal interpretation of the Force's will. By all means, entertain other perspectives on the Force—but remember that every effort must be taken to bring these beliefs under the guidance of the Jedi.

- The **Aing-Tii Monks** are among the most inscrutable of the galaxy's Force-users. These aliens inhabit the distant Kathol Rift and, through unknown means, are able to manipulate space for instantaneous teleportation. Those who have taken up residence near the Kathol Rift claim that the Aing-Tii can even visit other times and places through a discipline they call flow walking.

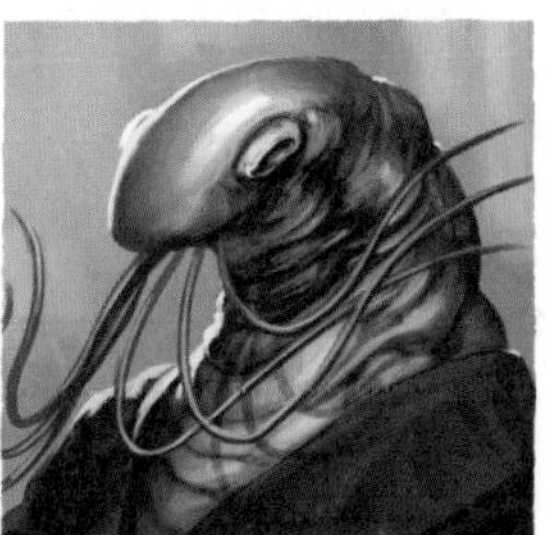

4.40 AING-TII MONK

- The **Baran Do Sages** of Dorin are the most gifted Force-users among the Kel Dor, and their reliance on breathing a helium atmosphere has not prevented members of their species from taking on great roles in the galaxy. Although a few Kel Dor have become Jedi, the Baran Do Sages use the Force to enhance their senses and perceive future events.

4.41 BARAN DO SAGE

4.42 Luka Sene

4.43 Matukai

4.44 Guardian of Breath

- On Alpheridies, the Miraluka perceive their environment through the Force to compensate for their natural blindness. The **Luka Sene** are a Miraluka sect that has achieved an unusually sharp perception of the world, while devoting themselves to study and knowledge.
- The **Matukai,** who have committed themselves to physical discipline, are among the best martial artists in existence. They achieve their mastery through a Force bond that strengthens their blows and refreshes their fighting spirit.
- The Kashi **Guardians of Breath** still persist, despite the ancient destruction of their homeworld by a supernova. Blessed with a strong connection to the Living Force, their scattered members can stimulate remarkable surges in the cell growth of both plants and animals.

I fought a Matukai—never again! —Thame

I THINK I LIKE THIS GUY THAME—WOULDN'T WANT TO FACE THEM EITHER. —AHSOKA

Fascinating! Q-G

MANY MATUKAI HAVE JOINED MY ORDER, BUT THEY PREFER TO DISTINGUISH THEMSELVES WITH A FACIAL TATTOO. —LUKE

Can't wait—so much I can teach!
-Thame

TAKING ON A PADAWAN LEARNER

IF ONLY YOU HAD SPENT MORE TIME LEARNING THE FUNDAMENTALS, MASTER.
—DOOKU

BY GRAND MASTER FAE COVEN

Although it is not mandatory, at some point during your knighthood, you may feel the desire to pass on your knowledge to another, younger Jedi. As a Jedi Knight you are encouraged to heed the Force's call, particularly if you sense it is leading you toward mentorship. Aside from recruitment, this is the most important action you can take to ensure that our Order remains vibrant and strong. Taking a Padawan apprentice will complete the cycle that first brought you to knighthood, and if concluded successfully will elevate you to the rank of Jedi Master.

Master Dooku is an intimidating mentor. That's not how I'm going to do it.
Q-G

4.45 MEMBERS OF THE TEMPLE STAFF CAN ANSWER QUESTIONS ABOUT PROMISING STUDENTS.

HE must be joking. Master Qui-Gon intimidates everyone!
-Kenobi

If you wish to select a student, visit the Temple. Each year during the Apprentice Tournaments our older Initiates demonstrate their fitness with lightsabers, but you are free to visit at any time to observe classes or to question the Temple's instructors. Remember that you once underwent the same process, so as you experience it from the other side, be mindful of what you felt and learned those many years ago.

Your apprentice should be much like you in temperament and outlook, but not *too* much alike. The teaching process is bidirectional, and you should expect to learn much from

4.46 Taking an apprentice continues the cycle that sustains the Jedi Order.

OBI-WAN FOLLOWS THE RULES A LITTLE TOO CLOSELY. THERE ARE A LOT OF TEMPLE TEACHINGS I COULD CORRECT.
Anakin

GREAT, SO I'M THE ONE WHO GETS IN TROUBLE?
-AHSOKA

your student. A fresh perspective and a second set of eyes will help you succeed on missions that would have been impossible for you alone. Don't forget that your Padawan has the benefit of recent Temple teachings, which you may have never studied. Keep an open mind and you will fuel the development of your shared Force bond.

Above all, do not be overprotective! Your Padawan may be young, but he or she is a Jedi. Better that you should lose your Padawan to tragedy than to avoid danger altogether. Every member of the Jedi Order is prepared to die in the service of the Republic—any lesser commitment is selfishness and waste.

YES—BETTER TO LEARN THE TRUTH OF THE WORLD.
—DOOKU

On this we agree!
Q-G

While taking on a Padawan is a step most Jedi will accept, some will choose to never have an apprentice. Not all Jedi possess the patience for what is a full-time commitment that can last a decade or more. Still others may have the desire but do not find a Padawan that suits their pace and outlook.

Meditate intensely before making a decision. It is far better to pass over this opportunity than to accept it out of duty. A poor fit with your Padawan will lead to poor instruction, squander your time, and leave your apprentice ill-prepared to face the Trials.

Becoming a Master and Grand Master

By Grand Master Fae Coven

The rank of Jedi Master is the highest formal recognition one can achieve in the Jedi Order. It is not a requirement, nor does it mark the end of your journey. Jedi who have attained this rank are the fewest in membership, and are outnumbered by even the younglings.

4.47 Your Padawan's transition to knighthood may also elevate you to the rank of Master.

Masters are known for their mentorship of younger Jedi. Taking on and training a Padawan into knighthood is one step toward attaining the rank of Master. Many Masters take on one Padawan after another, selecting an apprentice immediately following the previous apprentice's passing of the Trials. However, not all Knights will choose to follow this path.

Jedi Knights who have shown extraordinary service to the Republic are sometimes appointed Masters through the special dispensation of the High Council. In addition, Jedi Knights may elect to undergo a modified, more challenging version of the Trials of Knighthood, which, if passed, has often been accepted as a mark of mastery.

As a Jedi Master, your missions will not fundamentally change. You are still responsible for aiding the needy and extending the Order's reach throughout the Republic. Yet because your Jedi skills will have deepened since your first solo mission as a Knight, you may also wish to consider a teaching role that suits your talents. The Temple and our satellite academies have need of Force philosophers, battlemasters, historians, and scientists, as well as experts in the peculiar obsessions of the Jedi Sentinels.

4.48 **Grand Master Fae Coven**

Grand Master is a title bestowed upon the greatest of all Masters, those who have been recognized as such by the members of the Order and ratified through the unanimous decision of the High Council. In the past, several Masters have held the title simultaneously and in essence created an elite guild.

The elected leader of the High Council, "Master of the Order" we call. This title a Grand Master often holds.

—Yoda

Currently only a single Jedi can be appointed Grand Master at any one time. I am quite happy to hold the title, so I trust you younger ones will indulge me if I don't announce plans to relinquish it anytime soon.

Transcending Death

By Grand Master Fae Coven

One day you will die, in battle or in your sleep, having lived the noble life of a Jedi. None can state with clarity what awaits after you become one with the Force, but your journey into the Netherworld will be instantaneous.

The Whills...? G-G

Some Sages among the Whills believe otherwise, holding out the possibility of existence in this world even after Jedi have shed their physical forms. Existing as luminous beings, such Jedi could retain the identities they held before death, but they would be unable to interact with the physical world. However, the idea of this existence stems from stories and theories—not reality.

Though we believe that all things are possible through the Force, as physical beings we are grounded, and our understanding has limits. Instead, think of these stories as metaphors for the Jedi Code's final precept: *There is no death, there is the Force.*

I first sensed Ben in this state, then Yoda and my father. It meant so much to see them, but there seems to be a limit to how long a spirit can tether itself to the living. I'm surprised that the Jedi of this era dismissed this ability as mere legend. So far the Holocrons I've acquired have contained references to Jedi even more ancient, including Galong-Tal, Plautopseum, and Arca Jeth. All are said to have passed into the Force while remaining behind in this world as phantoms, achieving this extreme transformation through the sublimation of a body's organic cells into a state of pure energy.

FROM MY OWN EXPERIENCE, I KNOW THAT FORCE SPIRITS CAN COMMUNICATE WITH THOSE STILL ALIVE, AND CAN APPEAR AS A VISION OF THEIR FORMER SELVES UNMARKED BY DISEASE OR INJURY. THEY CAN APPEAR ANYWHERE IN THE GALAXY TO THOSE WHO HAD KNOWN THEM IN LIFE—OR ECHO IN ONE'S THOUGHTS, AS BEN DID IN MINE. I'M CONTINUING A DEEP STUDY INTO THE DATA LAYERS OF THE KRIMSAN HOLOCRON. THERE IS MUCH MORE GOING ON HERE THAN THEORY.

—LUKE

Library of Congress Cataloging-in-Publication Data available.
ISBN: 978-1-4521-0227-6

The Jedi Path: A Manual for Students of the Force is produced by becker&mayer!
11120 NE 33rd Place, Suite 101
Bellevue, Washington 98004
www.beckermayer.com

Edited by Delia Greve
Designed by Rosanna Brockley
Production coordination by Jen Marx

Lucasfilm Ltd.
Executive Editor: J.W. Rinzler
Art Director: Troy Alders
Keeper of the Holocron: Leland Chee
Director of Publishing: Carol Roeder
www.starwars.com

Manufactured in China

Text and annotations written by Daniel Wallace
Illustrations by: Paul Allan Ballard: 2.1 – 2.4, 2.6, 2.7. 2.20 – 2.22; Jeff Carlisle: 3.14, 3.66, 3.67, 4.1, 4.6; Tommy Lee Edwards: 2.27 – 2.30, 3.25 – 3.27, 3.29 – 3.37, 4.29, 4.30; Ryan Hobson: 2.13, 3.28, annotation sketch p.109, 4.27, 4.28, annotation sketch p. 159; Greg Knight: 3.15, 3.78,4.5, 4.23 – 4.25; Chris Reiff: 2.15, 3.18, 3.19, 3.43, 4.34, 4.35; Derek Thompson: 2.8, 2.16 – 2.19, 3.47 – 3.58, 3.70, 4.20, 4.21, 4.36 – 4.38; Chris Trevas: 1.2, 2.23, 2.24, 3.17, 3.44; Terryl Whitlatch: 3.59 – 3.65; Kieran Yanner: 3.71 – 3.76, 4.26, 4.45 – 4.47; Conceptopolis, LLC: 1.1, 1.3 – 1.6. 2.10 – 2.12, 2.14, 2.25, 2.26, 3.9 – 3.13, 3.16, 3.20 – 3.24, 4.7, 4.48; Storm Lion Pte Ltd: 2.9, 2.31, 3.1 – 3.7, 3.38 – 3.42, 3.45, 3.46, 3.68, 3.69, 3.77, 3.79, 4.2 – 4.4, 4.8 – 4.19, 4.22, 4.31, 4.32, 4.39 – 4.44

10 9 8

Chronicle Books LLC
680 Second Street
San Francisco, California 94107

www.chroniclebooks.com